IGNORANT ARMIES

Sam Wharton

The Second Novel in the Jonathan Hare Trilogy

Published by

An Imprint of Melrose Press Limited
St Thomas Place, Ely
Cambridgeshire
CB7 4GG, UK
www.melrosebooks.com

FIRST EDITION

Cover designed by Jeremy Kay

ISBN 978 1 907040 93 1

Printed and bound in Great Britain by:
CLE Digital Solutions. St Ives, Cambridgeshire

FSC
Mixed Sources
Product group from well-managed
forests and other controlled sources
Cert no. TT-COC-003115
www.fsc.org
© 1996 Forest Stewardship Council

Dedication

For my lovely wife Jackie, who listened patiently as I struggled to write this story and who made such helpful suggestions.

Foreword

The three novels that make up the Hare Trilogy have a lot to do with my experiences in England after World War II. I based Jonathan's clandestine skills on a demonstration of locksmithing and safe-breaking I witnessed during a diplomatic briefing in a secret underground location in London in 1967. His fascination with camouflage and magic tricks mirrors my own.

The setting of the stories is based on historical facts; there were landed and titled families wielding untrammelled power and there was a form of warfare between those on the extreme Left politically and those accustomed to exercising power – referred to as the Establishment. So severe was this warfare, that by 1956 one landed estate with its ancestral home was being demolished or sold off every single day, some will say for the better.

What Jonathan discovers is that the warfare was painful for all concerned.

Contents

Preface

THIS IS THE SECOND STORY ABOUT JONATHAN Hare, a young man growing up in the 1950s in England.

In the first story, *Passe Partout*, Jonathan has just completed his boarding school education with an academic record qualifying him for University. But he has another talent; he is an exceptional safe-breaker.

It is 1954, a time of great social upheaval caused by the Labour government's imposition of extreme left wing legislation. The forces of the Establishment try to hold back the tidal wave of changes and Jonathan finds himself caught up in the consequent, but unacknowledged class war. Both sides want to employ his special talents and he has to choose. He is sent to an aristocratic family facing financial ruin to open a safe that has defeated all other experts. While he is trying to open the safe, he naively thinks that the family has accepted him. After he succeeds, he is devastated when he is summarily dismissed and sent away, back to his working class home.

Along the way, Jonathan has met many people in positions of power; some are Establishment figures, some are career criminals. He has made friends and enemies that will continue to shape his life.

As *Ignorant Armies* begins, he is still licking his wounds, unable to focus on a Scholarship opportunity to a new College that has just been opened in Oxford University.

ONE

Ignorant Armies

JONATHAN HARE SAT STARING OUT OF HIS attic window in a black mood. He had rescued an aristocratic family from financial ruin and, for his efforts, had been coldly dismissed. He replayed the scene in the Great Study for the hundredth time. Eventually it dawned on him that the dismissal had been staged, even decided upon beforehand. He came to with a start.

A voice from the past was saying 'Stop whining, Hare, and get on with it'. He smiled; it was the Housemaster everyone knew as 'The Toad' growling at him as he lay on the rugby field nursing his knee. His Oxford University Entrance results were good enough to get him on the short list for the Galdraith Scholarship. So he would concentrate on that; if he won it, he would be his own man with a promising future.

Oxford University was slumbering through the summer of 1954 just as it had for hundreds of years before. It has been home to people famous in the arts and sciences, among them the poet Matthew Arnold. In the middle of the nineteenth century he wrote *On Dover Beach*. The last two verses read:

> *Ah, love, let us be true*
> *To one another! for the world, which seems*
> *To lie before us like a land of dreams,*
> *So various, so beautiful, so new,*
> *Hath really neither joy, nor love, nor light,*

1

Nor certitude, nor peace, nor help for pain;
And we are here as on a darkling plain
Swept with confused alarms of struggle and flight,
Where ignorant armies clash by night.

No one knows what inspired Arnold's sombre mood but had he been writing in Jonathan's day it might have been a reaction to the class warfare that came to a head after the General Election of 1945. Minimum wage legislation was imposed and those accustomed to power watched as one landed estate after another became unsupportable[1]. So they decided to fight a rearguard action against such radical social changes. It was a dark period in the life of England for there could be no compromise. As in all warfare, when decisions are based on wilful ignorance of the enemy's strength, tragic results follow. By 1954 the battle lines of the Great Class War were well established and Jonathan had already been drawn into the fray[2].

---

1   By 1956 one such ancestral home was being demolished or sold off every day.

2   His experiences are described in the novel *Passe Partout.*

Two

City of Dreaming Spires

THE CITY OF OXFORD LIES JUST A few miles north of Jonathan's hometown. It is so full of historic architectural wonders that it is known throughout the world as 'the city of dreaming spires'[3]. About fifty miles west of London, it has been home to the University of Oxford for some nine hundred years. The City of Cambridge has a University to rival it, not quite so old perhaps, but with just as enviable a reputation. It has long been accepted by the 'Establishment[4]' that a good 'Oxbridge'[5] degree is essential to any worthwhile career.

In 1954, the two Universities represented what was good and what was bad about higher education in England. Some Colleges had been patronized for centuries by the Royals, by aristocrats and by the well positioned. Some Colleges had become virtually the private domain of these families, and their children would be educated there as a matter of course. That an influential career would result was simply the natural order of things.

Both Universities produced fast stream entrants into the Civil Service, particularly the Foreign Office, and provided fertile ground

---

3   Matthew Arnold also coined this phrase in an otherwise forgotten poem.
4   A derogatory term coined by the political Left to describe those exercising power through family influence rather than merit.
5   An unofficial but well accepted term for either Oxford or Cambridge, exclusive of all other places of higher learning.

for recruitment into the more clandestine agencies of government[6]. In 1859, the powers that be decided that the Universities were appropriate places to locate Officer Training Corps units.

The interview for the Galdraith Scholarship was only a day or two away. Jonathan knew he ought to be preparing for it, even if his anger kept returning and he was finding it hard to concentrate. Gritting his teeth, he got his bike out of the shed and went up to the jerry-built library to see if he could unearth something about the Scholarship. To his surprise, the woman at the librarian's desk recognized the name 'Galdraith'.

"Oh yes," she said with a wintry smile. "It's the title chosen by our local hero, Mr. William Magnette, the industrialist, you know. Lord Galdraith now, if you please, sponsored that new College at Oxford, didn't he? Wants to focus on science and the like. Looked down on by the University, of course; anything less than five hundred years old is just trop nouveau!"

Her accent was appalling, but Jonathan got the point.

"Let me see your library card, please," she asked, getting up from behind the desk. She inspected the one that his mother let him use.

"Don't you have a card of your own?"

Jonathan explained that he was hardly ever in the town, "Boarding school, you know, then I'm going up in September."

She looked at him with sudden interest. "To Oxford?"

He nodded.

"Let me give you a research card; we don't get many undergraduates in here," she said, giving him a special smile.

"Come back tomorrow and I'll have something about Lord Galdraith for you."

As he walked out of the Library, he remembered that it was here that he first met Victoria. He sighed; her mother had soon put a stop to

---

6   Burgess and McLean who defected to the Soviets are two arch examples; both were recruited from Cambridge.

that. When he got home, his eyes fell once more on the blue envelope that he had brought back from London. He didn't need to look at it again, for all it contained was a cutting from the *Tatler* announcing that Victoria's marriage 'would not now take place'. There was nothing else. Part of him was glad that she hadn't added anything; the other part wondered what had happened to her. But that was a closed chapter; her family had made sure of that, so he must put it behind him and get on with his life.

The next day Jonathan collected the material on Lord Galdraith from the librarian and mulled it over. It was surprisingly comprehensive, but the portrayal of William Magnette, now Lord Galdraith, was unflattering. The industrialist had made his money the hard way, and had bought his title with strategic donations to approved causes. The more Jonathan read the material, the more he sensed the same antagonism that had permeated those idiotic lectures at St. Eligius, the sixth-form College that he had gone to after Standish and where he had prepared for his University Entrance Exams. He put down the Galdraith material and thought about why it should be so swingeing in its criticism; all he could come up with was that the librarian must be a left wing loony, although she hadn't looked like one – she didn't have wire-rimmed granny glasses or dirty braided hair. He realised that if he focused on the facts and ignored the commentary there was a lot of useful information. She had even included a newspaper cutting showing Lord Galdraith standing at the gates of Buckingham Palace celebrating his Peerage.

Charles Barnes, Jonathan's friend and classmate at St. Eligius, had also completed his Summer Assignment. He had been found a place at Scotland Yard, home of the Metropolitan Police, where his service as a temporary police cadet in the Commissioner's special programme had earmarked him for the fast-stream. But thanks to Jonathan's coaching in exam technique Charles had also succeeded in getting a place at

London University, where he would specialize in a new programme, Modern Management Techniques. His assignment over, he was heading home.

Deep in his reading, Jonathan hardly heard the rapping on the front door. He was surprised to find Charles there. He had avoided bringing any of his friends to the terraced house before, but Charles just looked around and smiled.

"Another Railway house; they must have built hundreds of these. Nothing special, but comfortable enough!"

Jonathan relaxed, saying with a smile, "You should have seen our place in Cornwall – no gas, no electricity, earth privy at the bottom of the garden, nearest telephone a mile and a half away! This place is luxury compared to that."

Charles made some small talk, trying to assess Jonathan's state of mind and wondering how to open the subject. He told himself to dive straight in.

"Do you remember where I was assigned this summer?"

"Just a moment," Jonathan said, thinking hard. "Wasn't it some-where in Scotland?"

Charles laughed. "Same old Jonathan, it was Scotland Yard, the Metropolitan Police, you dunce! I was there when you were up to your high jinks with Harry[7]."

He told Jonathan about being a collator for the all-out police operation against the Grey Gang, and how he had pieced together the train of events that Jonathan had started that night in old Bronsky's pawnshop.

"I couldn't believe how you were cheated of the credit, and then set up as a link to the Gang. Did you know you were under surveillance?"

Jonathan explained how he had spotted Sergeant Davies' car, the black Wolsley.

---

7   Harry Sparrow, Jonathan's mentor during his time in London.

Charles shook his head, "Oh no, that must have been another agency; I never saw any reports from them!"

Jonathan was starting to feel nervous. "You mean there were others watching me?"

Charles laughed. "Dozens of them, no expense spared; you nearly destroyed some careers with that disguise when you went to the Savoy."

Jonathan had to sit down; he found he was sweating.

"Disguise? You mean the hat?"

"Not just the hat, but that spiffy suit as well."

Jonathan finally smiled.

"Well, I did get a hat from old Bronsky, a present to go with the suit. The old man was so grateful for clearing Ronnie[8] out of his shop; it was embarrassing really. Anyway, you have to wear a hat in the West End; you'd look out of place otherwise."

Charles decided to press on.

"Then you went in to the Savoy. That took the team by surprise I can tell you. And you were seen in the company of a high class young lady, seemed you knew her well, took her away out of sight of our man. That really threw everyone off the scent for a while, especially me."

Jonathan recalled how pretty Victoria had looked in her finery. He hadn't expected to see her and her public recognition of him had been dangerous. He had reacted so strongly that he was sure she would never speak to him again.

Charles was facing some new hurdles. He saw no sense in stopping now.

"It was then that I got the feeling that you were being used for something too important for the likes of us to know about. I never got the whole thing, but there was some liaison with other services. I never saw anything on the files because information was being

---

8   Ronnie Grey, modelled on one of the infamous Kray twins who terrorized London.

fed directly to the Commissioner[9]. Sir Hubert's a cagey one, easy to underestimate. I don't expect you to tell me what they asked you to do; I do know that it must have involved some really important people."

Jonathan had a distant look in his eyes; Charles waited for some sign from him.

Jonathan finally said, "Well, yes, you're right, all a bit painful really; rather not talk about it."

"Ah," said Charles, "My guess is that they turned against you when you had done your job."

Jonathan couldn't hide his astonishment. "How on earth did you work that out?"

Charles admitted that it was an educated guess based on his opinion of the people in high society. And he had this Statement of Offences to support his view. He hoped it wouldn't be too much of a shock for Jonathan.

"I want you to have this, but you must never say how you got it; it would stop my career dead in its tracks if they ever found out," he said, taking the envelope out of his inside pocket.

Jonathan opened the envelope and took out the piece of paper and unfolded it. He read:

---

9   Sir Hubert de Quincy.

DPS _____

Metropolitan Police
Statement of Offences

Subject – Jonathan Hare alias Samuel Ward

Whereas the subject is an associate of the Grey Gang who had fallen out with Ronald Grey, a Gang leader, then under surveillance by Task Force 21; and,

Whereas the feud came to a head in the 'King's Head Public House', when the Task Force was able to capture Ronald Grey while he was exacting revenge on the subject; and,

Whereas the subject is a skilled housebreaker and an expert in safe-breaking, having been trained by the Gang in these skills; and,

Whereas he is recorded as trying to branch out on his own assuming the name of Samuel Ward; and,

Whereas he is known to frequent the operational headquarters of the Gang at 12 Thames Street, Millwall in the Isle of Dogs,

Now therefore he is charged as follows:

Offence 1: Kidnapping Lady Jane Bellestream from Mountbeck, Heckmondsley, Yorkshire, in the company of a well known Gang member, Sailor Wilson,

Offence 2: Confining the aforesaid in the warehouse at 12 Thames Street, Millwall.

Caution: The suspect has evaded the police and is now at large, whereabouts unknown.

MP SO-4

Charles watched Jonathan turn several shades whiter, and said quickly, "Now, Jonathan, it's not as bad as it looks. It would never stand up in Court, and I know for a fact that it was never logged into the system. See, it should have a red number issued by the Prosecution[10] people here in the upper right corner. Someone had this prepared to silence you if it became necessary. I had to let you know how ruthless the people are who employed you. I know this isn't your style at all!"

Jonathan felt pole-axed; being thrown out like an old shoe was bad enough but now he was being attacked by someone with power. His boarding school resolve hardly equipped him to deal with this sort of danger. He was trying hard to get his stone face in place when he realised that he didn't have to hide from Charles.

"It was all so straightforward, the job I mean, just open a safe that no one else could. The kidnapping wasn't my idea; the first thing I knew Lady Jane and I were trapped in a car with Sailor Wilson, roaring down to London to meet Arthur Salmon[11]. Even Sailor didn't like it; poor idiot is going to rot in jail forever. Did you know how much he helped us capture the Gang? I bet he didn't get any credit for it either."

Charles was fascinated, and encouraged Jonathan to talk. He learned about the warehouse and smiled. "Yes, I worked that out, told the Commissioner that they would take you there. You had opened a safe there earlier, hadn't you?"

Jonathan nodded.

"And the Gang wouldn't have called you in unless the safe was really important, so it had to be at their headquarters!" said Charles.

Jonathan gave him an admiring glance, and explained how he had fooled Freddy, the guard on the door, and how Lady Jane and he had escaped. Charles was stumped by the mechanics of the escape, so Jonathan explained the magician's cabinet trick that made Freddy think they had gone out of the loading doors.

---

10   The Directorate of Prosecution Services numbers were prefixed by 'DPS'.
11   Acting head of the Grey Gang following Ronnie's capture. Reggie, the other twin, was already in prison.

Charles was flabbergasted. "Wait a minute, you mean like where the girl is in the cabinet, but can't be there really because of the swords pushed through, and yet there she is when the door is opened?"

"But the other way round," Jonathan agreed.

They laughed about it, much to Charles' relief. He had worried that Jonathan wouldn't be able to take the shock of the Statement of Offences, but he seemed to have got over it.

Charles looked at his watch. "My train is due soon; my parents will be waiting for me; it'll be good to be home for a few days!"

Charles had been gone for several minutes before Jonathan realised the significance of what he had said about Sergeant Davies. So it must have been Sir Roger[12] personally who had been feeding Sir Hubert the information. He picked up the Statement of Offences document. If someone in authority wanted to threaten him, this would be an excellent way to do it. If Charles hadn't told him about the failure to log it in and the lack of that number, he would have taken it at face value, in which case it would have caused the bravest heart to beat faster. He wondered what sort of authority would be needed to prepare the document. There was something strange about the choice of words, too. 'Exacting revenge' and 'frequent the operational headquarters of the Gang' sounded too grandiose for such a document.

"Sounds more like the stuff put out to glorify the Commissioner," he said to himself.

Eventually his musing about the necessary authority and the Commissioner's liking for publicity came together in his mind. He put the document down with the realisation that it had to have been prepared under Sir Hubert's orders, probably with the prompting of his brother, Sir Roger. But why hadn't they used it against him?

He cast his mind back to the evening before he had opened the Mountbeck safe. He had been tired after the excitement of the escape from the Gang and had not fully understood Sir Roger's probing. They

---

12   Sir Roger de Quincy, head of an agency set up to support the 'Establishment' side of the Class War.

had talked about the kidnapping and he had told Sir Roger that 'whoever had organized it ought to be made to pay the price'.

Sir Roger, he realised now, had reacted unusually. Jonathan had become used to his smoothness and quickness of mind, but Sir Roger had turned white and swallowed several times before he changed the subject abruptly. And then he had walked out of the room without as much as a 'thank you' or a handshake.

Jonathan sighed, aware now that he did have enemies and highly placed ones at that. His resolve returned; he must put all this out of his mind and make sure he won the Scholarship. Then he would be safe, he thought.

Three

The Aftermath

I F JONATHAN WAS FINDING IT DIFFICULT TO put his recent experience behind him, so were others. Colin Davies, recently promoted to Inspector, had been Jonathan's minder under orders from Sir Roger de Quincy. He was getting worried by the increasing evidence that his boss was not himself. Colin had been impressed by Sir Roger's coolness during the many operations they had conducted. There had been some failures to be sure, but Colin was proud of the smooth way that their operation could identify and counter the more underhanded means by which the Movement[13] attacked those whose only crime was to be landed and titled.

Something had happened in the operation to round up the Grey Gang that had triggered the change. Colin had never been part of anything like it before; he had thought that it was going to be a simple task of minding Hare so that he could open that safe at Mountbeck. To be sure the Movement had tried its best to bring the Bellestream family down, but it had always been a clandestine attack on the family's assets, a typical Bessemer action, sinister perhaps but never violent.

No one at Mountbeck had been concerned about young Lady Jane getting in the car with the Hare lad; they were only going on a social visit after all. But the car had been a trap set by the Grey Gang, grabbing Hare to take him to London for some form of retribution. Once it was realised

---

13   The Bessemer Movement, the unofficial name for the organization set up by left wing activists to 'bring the Establishment to its knees'.

that Lady Jane was in the Gang's hands, however, all hell broke loose. It was only Hare's ingenuity that had saved their bacon, for the Bellestream family were the friends of the most powerful people in the Establishment. In fact, if Colin had read the situation correctly, Sir Roger had been under pressure from the Palace; he shivered at the thought of the consequences if the Gang's operation had harmed Lady Jane.

It was on the return journey from Mountbeck that Colin noticed that all was not well with Sir Roger. He had come out of the great entrance in a rush, most unusual for him. His face was grey, and he hadn't said a word, just gestured to drive away. Colin had thought for a moment that Sir Roger was sweating, but surely not?

Roger was only too aware that he and his brother Hubert had escaped by the skin of their teeth. They had devised an elaborate plan to prompt the Gang to kidnap Hare, hoping to track them to the Gang's headquarters deep in that desolate area known as the Isle of Dogs. They weren't unduly worried about Hare's fate; they calculated that the importance of capturing the Gang far outweighed that risk. They never envisioned that Lady Jane would decide to accompany Hare and that immediately put them in a perilous position; jeopardizing one of the Bellestreams would never be accepted by a Certain Person. After all, it had been made clear by a Messenger that the Bellestreams had to be protected.

The problem was that although everything had worked out in the end, Hare knew that it was the two of them that had engineered the kidnapping. And it had been Hare, of all people, who had apparently got Jane out of the trap. Roger hadn't understood the stagecraft that Hare had used. His brother had dismissed the lad's explanation as preposterous; he preferred to think that Hare had some favours to cash in and had been set free by 'one of his cronies'. Roger knew that his brother had by now made himself fireproof, for this was a necessary skill if one wanted to remain in the post of Commissioner.

But Hare still had knowledge that could bring them down so the two of them had concocted a plan to silence him. They had a document created that would appear official enough to frighten the young man, but only they would know of its existence. It would be impossible to process it through the official Prosecution channels for fear of letting others into the secret.

What was really eating away at Roger was something about the Hare person. His wife had met Jonathan a couple of years earlier and had commented that he was 'the spitting image of you as a young man'. And there had been several occasions when he had noticed this himself. Perhaps this was why, when he had the opportunity to give Hare the document and frighten him into silence, he had been unable to deliver the coup. It was a weakness that he could not resolve and it was eroding his self-confidence. Several times recently he had lost his temper over matters of no consequence; and his alcohol consumption had increased a lot, he thought with a wry smile.

Superintendent Alistair Henderson had been head of the Serious Crimes Division at Scotland Yard for the last year. It was certainly not a promotion that he had sought, for he hadn't initially relished working so closely with the Commissioner. Had he known the Commissioner better, he would have realised that it was that independent streak coupled with his Edinburgh degree that had secured him the promotion.

The public had been particularly affronted by the ease with which the Grey Gang had got Ronnie out of Pentonville, and the Press had taken the opportunity to flail at the authorities. Recapture of Ronnie had become the Division's top priority and the Commissioner had notched up the pressure. But the Gang had virtually annexed the Dockland area and it was such a no-go area that, despite the use of massive resources, the police couldn't track Ronnie's movements. So it had been a major success when they were able to recapture him in that huge East End pub and the Commissioner had played it up for all it was worth. Several members of the Division received promotions and awards, and it hadn't done his career prospects any harm, either.

This was only the first of the startling successes that his Division had achieved during the summer. While these triumphs had certainly been gratifying, he had recently begun to be unsettled about them. Alistair's Scots upbringing had taught him that success had to be earned by hard work. So he found it impossible to gloat, for there had been something too fortuitous, too unearned about the recapture of Ronnie, who must have been mad to go barging into that pub just outside the fringes of Dockland.

And then there was the strange tale told about Harry Sparrow's new apprentice, whom Harry called Ward. His doubts had been reinforced by the Commissioner's instincts about the young man and Alistair had taken it upon himself to apply watching resources. First they discovered that his name wasn't Ward, it was Hare, and that he had come armed with exceptional skills as a locksmith and in safe-breaking.

Then they had picked up something that really sparked his interest. Hare had been spotted going back to the Royal Horological Society[14] without Harry, and, well, Alistair was no fool, it obviously signalled something of major importance. He knew better than to pursue any inquiries into what went on *there*, sure to end a career, as everyone of his rank knew. It was lucky for him that he had some rapport with Colin Davies and could confirm, although never directly, the intelligence that was coming in to Sir Hubert almost daily. That it came from the Commissioner's brother would never be established, but Alistair was confident that the two had put aside their differences over a matter of such national importance.

He had watched with fascination as Sir Hubert pieced together an interpretation of the events surrounding Ronnie's capture and had been mildly shocked when the Commissioner had concluded that the Hare fellow was associated with the Gang. Alistair couldn't see any logic in that idea, but decided not to voice his doubts, certainly not in front of the other members present in Grey Central – he smiled with private amusement at Sir Hubert's insistence on calling the converted Third Floor Briefing Room by such a grandiose term.

---

14   The front for the Agency set up to protect the Establishment from the Bessemer Movement

But he had to take his hat off to Sir Hubert, for the room had played an important part in later events, culminating in that traumatic action to capture the remaining Gang leaders. Once more a sense of unease descended on the superintendent, for he found it simply too facile an explanation that Arthur had kidnapped this Hare lad in order to demonstrate his overall control. He had felt sure that Arthur had some other agenda, and when Forensics finally reported that the horribly disfigured body that the Thames Police had recovered was none other than Bert Coleman, Arthur's bookkeeper, Alistair saw another explanation. He had put a seal on the report, severely limiting its circulation; he had needed all his authority as superintendent to pull that off, he remembered. Colin Davies had previously felt free to tell him that Harry and Hare had done a job in that warehouse for Bert, and Alistair now felt sure that Hare had opened Arthur's safe and found out something that Arthur couldn't afford to become public knowledge. He kept this idea to himself.

He had never previously seen any sign in Sir Hubert of anxiety or stress, anger certainly and impatience often, but the whole campaign to round up the Grey Gang had suddenly developed a strange undertone of, well, perhaps not panic, but something like it. And then, out of the shadows Sir Roger appeared, invited to witness the triumph, or so Sir Hubert had intimated, but it hadn't looked quite like that to Alistair. And after the frantic efforts to rescue that young Lady Jane came the moment when Colin Davies and Hare had been brought to the Yard. Alistair had expected to be present, but the emergency requiring his attention had turned out to be a hoax. So he only heard rumours of the way the two so-called heroes had been shuffled off into the background. The list of medals and minor honours which had been approved and which would be published a suitable time after the media attention had died down included neither.

And, Alistair realised, it was soon after that that he had noticed the iciness whenever Hare's name turned up. He shook his head; perhaps there was nothing in this to warrant his ruminations. No, he thought, trust your instincts. And, for all the involvement of the Hare lad, he still hadn't met him; perhaps he should put that on his priority list.

He had to put these thoughts aside, for the Commissioner was suddenly taken up with a different threat. Intelligence was being received that American interests were trying to get a foothold in the gambling world and Alistair didn't need the Commissioner to explain the long-term implications of that. There was quite enough gambling going on already, but this threat seemed to be aimed at the players in the higher social circles.

The Headmaster at St. Eligius School was nervously hosting a meeting with the Bessemer Movement's chief executive, a massively built ex-steelworker from the north of England, whose ability to reduce otherwise mature and sensible men to quivering wrecks was a legend.

The Movement had established itself in the late eighteenth century as an activist organization that had as its aim the overthrow of the very people that had invested in the facilities that had brought the Industrial Revolution its world fame. The activism had, in a clandestine way, engineered the slow but successful rise to political power of the Labour movement in the early twentieth century. They were particularly proud of supporting financial measures to curb the power of the Establishment, introduced with the sinister title of 'Death Duties'.

These measures and the death in the two World Wars of many of those who would have taken over the management of these sometimes massive empires had seen to it that this privileged way of life was seriously threatened.

But the Movement contributed to the attack on the Establishment in another way. They equipped graduates of their College, St. Eligius, with skills that helped them to expose and take advantage of weaknesses within that society. While the movement was careful not to condone anything illegal, it had to be said that St. Eligius graduates were eased into positions in which their knowledge of certain arcane skills was always to the detriment of those in the Establishment.

The Movement had long coveted one of the Bellestream's most attractive holdings, called the Abercorn, for development and profit. That it would remove some of the estate's landholdings was an added bonus. They had thought that Lord Erinmore's period of incompetence would create a favourable climate in which to acquire the Abercorn at a bargain price. The news that his Lordship was recovering and might, if he got that safe open, get access to enough wealth to avoid the sale, came as a shock, and had caused them to send Jonathan there to open the safe with the object of taking custody of any valuable resources that were thought to languish there. The Movement considered this to be his duty in return for his education at St. Eligius. But Jonathan's emergence from that school unmoved by the political indoctrination had gone unnoticed. All they knew was that Jonathan had delivered a package of assets to Harry Sparrow to take to the Movement.

The matter at hand, then, was the examination of the package. The Headmaster, alerted by Charles Barnes, had already briefed the Chief Executive on the possibility that Hare had been suborned by another agency perhaps acting for the Establishment. This had not gone down well, because the overpowering presence was accustomed to bulldozing aside such concerns.

"Look, this is exactly what we expected and is just what I ordered Hare to bring to us. I think we should be pleased with his performance. These assets will go into our war chest."

The matter appeared to be closed.

The Headmaster took a deep breath. "Will you take any cut-out measures?"

The silence that greeted this was ominous.

The Headmaster continued bravely, "I just have this feeling that a small investment in, shall we say, reconnaissance, might pay dividends."

The Chief Executive, for all his gruffness, was no fool. "You think Hare could pull off this sort of deception?" he asked, his heavy eyebrows signalling incredulity.

"No, I don't, but, if he *has* been turned by one of those services that we have been harmed by before, they could have tutored him and certainly prepared false documents. I have no way of knowing whether these are genuine, do you?"

The huge man granted this a few moments' thought. "Reckon it wouldn't cost us much."

It was as close to a concession as the Headmaster had ever heard.

Arthur Salmon had sunk into a depression. He may have avoided the fate of the other ringleaders captured in that raid, but it would look as if he had conspired with the police to set up the operation. He knew what Ronnie and Reggie would make of that.

He had got home late the night before the police raid, angry that he hadn't been able to deal with Hare. Flora had left him a note that someone had telephoned with a warning that the police were planning some major operation. Normally he would have discounted it knowing that the Gang was safe in its own territory, but there had been that code word 'Santa Nicola' that only a very few in his private world of illegal money transfers would have known. So he had taken some extra precautions and discovered that there was unusual activity on the Thames; more police launches than usual were out on the river and they were clustered too near the Isle of Dogs for his comfort. A few more phone calls revealed that another launch had been stationed on the Greenwich bank for longer than usual with its bow pointing directly at the warehouse.

Arthur may have been the financial brains behind the Gang, and ranked next after the twins, but he had never felt part of them. He had achieved his stature by concealing from them exactly how he managed to finance the illegal importation of all that contraband coming from offshore. He had needed help from a cartel on the Continent, but they had certainly benefited from the premiums he had to pay and he supposed that was why they had included him in their circle. It was in one of those meetings that he realised that the cartel took it for granted that he had an escape route. It dawned on him then that, however much care he took, and however safe he felt under the protection of the Gang, there was always a chance that something would go wrong.

The idea of escape had another attraction; his marriage to Flora had been a sham from the start. The twins had more or less arranged the marriage; their sister would never have found a suitor because no one in their right mind would want to become part of that family. It had provided Flora with the propriety that she craved. He smiled grimly at the picture of the thugs' sister so caught up in presenting a middle class appearance.

At the end of one of the meetings on the continent he had been taken into another room with two men he hadn't met before, Yanks by their accents and clothes. One was small and dark and did all the talking; the other said nothing, so Arthur knew that he was the muscle. The small man wanted to know about gambling in England. Arthur had an aversion to it himself, having watched so many go under chasing the odds on greyhounds and horses, a mug's game he thought; the punters could never accept that the bookies would always win in the end. He had no direct knowledge of what went on outside the East End, but everyone knew that there were clubs in Mayfair that catered to the toffs. The small man had taken this in with no expression on his face, but had shaken Arthur's hand afterwards, for rather too long Arthur had thought, but Yanks were like that, weren't they?

From time to time after that, Arthur had answered questions over the telephone from the States and eventually discovered that the small man went by the name of Joe. Then came the day when Joe asked him to find a property in Mayfair or close to it. Arthur was, well, flattered, he supposed; money was apparently of no importance whereas the specifications were precise to the point of obsession. He had found a suitable place and oversaw the acquisition and structural alterations through a couple of his private companies that the Gang would never know about. The company listed on the leasehold paperwork was only one of the many he had set up to siphon off some of the cash he handled. Another of his companies contracted with some interior decorators, awful pooves dancing around flapping their hands in the air, squeaking with delight. Then the gambling tables arrived and cameras and all sorts of other equipment. When it was finished, Arthur thought it looked like a done-up whore house, but what did he know?

So when Joe told him that the property needed a full time security person on the premises, Arthur decided that it would make a perfect bolthole.

He wandered around the luxurious surroundings, all a bit 'too-too' for him, free at last from Flora and from Ronnie and Reggie who were both 'inside' with most of the senior Gang members. The twins' reach, so effective once, was now unlikely to get to him. His new identity would buy him time, he hoped. All that doctored paperwork needed to pull off the currency transfers had put him in touch with the blacksmiths[15]; they had turned out to be more than useful in many other areas.

But, he asked himself, why don't I feel safe? At the back of his mind was the unfinished business with that fink Hare who had somehow got out of the warehouse, probably a stooge for the bill[16] all along. Hare knew what was stashed in the safe; he couldn't afford to have the secrets of his rake-off discovered by the twins. He'd have to deal with Hare once he felt more secure.

Edward Bellestream, Lord Erinmore to use his family title, rarely thought about how Hare had solved the riddle of the old Champion safe; after all Hare was really only a tradesman. The liquid assets that had been recovered from the safe were enabling him to tackle the restoration of the great house of Mountbeck with some vigour. The ancestral home of the Bellestreams was beginning to return to its former self. It had never been a warm and welcoming place, stuck out as it was on the edge of the Yorkshire Moors, but it would be far more presentable when the restoration was complete. And Edward was taken up with the implications of his new status; he would be confirmed as the fifteenth Duke of Hawksmoore

---

15   A less well-known term for those skilled in preparing false paperwork – a play on the word 'forge'.

16   One of many terms used in the rougher parts of London for the Police.

as soon as the College of Arms finalized the protocols. So he seldom gave any thought to what Hare had achieved.

What he did recall was the reaction of his friend Paul, Count Paolo Passaglietti, after he had dismissed Hare. Paul had pointed out that Hare had gone out of his way to befriend Jane, his difficult niece, and had even rescued her from the Grey Gang. Paul's passing shot was that Edward ought to realize that Jane had a crush on the young man and the dismissal was a decision that Edward would regret. Paul had left for Italy immediately after that, taking his beautiful sister with him, to Edward's sorrow.

Jane's deterioration seemed to justify Paul's unusually brusque remark. After Hare left, her mood had swung so dramatically from exhilaration to despair that the doctors had recommended recuperation in a sanatorium. Edward was lost in the medical language but gathered that there were some drugs that might control her instability. What irritated him most was her insistence on bringing Hare back. But of course that was impossible; the lad was quite unsuitable and as Roger de Quincy had said, the young man had too many tricks up his sleeve. He already knew far too much about Jane's illness, a secret that the Bellestreams needed to keep to themselves; Hare might still use that knowledge to insinuate himself into the family.

FOUR

Piece of Mind

Lady Antonia de Quincy, Elaine Worth on the stage, and Doris Fletcher before that, had arrived at the handsome house that was home to the Royal Horological Society. Antonia was accustomed to having her own way and had perfected certain postures in order to ensure an uninterrupted stream of personal satisfaction. She had been amazed at Victoria's rebellion, and all her guile had failed to change her daughter's mind. What a marriage that would have been – fancy, Victoria, Countess of Dornoch, how many doors that would have opened!

Her own title was nice, but she had sensed that in so-called polite society she was tolerated rather than accepted. She had overheard someone say that the wife of a Baronet is really only a jumped-up commoner, and had become used to the way conversations seemed to die whenever she joined a group.

Roger, however, was able to rise above such pettiness, although she had never fathomed how he did it. Even Royal Dukes might be seen chatting comfortably with him, and not just at those awful Garden Parties either.

She had given up a promising stage career when Roger married her, and she saw nothing wrong in using dramatic devices to further her own interests. Roger presumably knew what he was doing, although why he had appeared so soon after Victoria's birth with that offer, quite out of the blue, she had never discovered. Since he had a title and money and was so well-mannered, a little remote perhaps, but never harsh, she had decided that it was a move in her best interests, particularly since Victoria would present such difficulties in the life of a star of the stage.

It had never occurred to her that others in that world considered her outrageous beauty her only asset. Her stage presence was florid and Victorian and not at all what directors wanted nowadays. Perhaps when she was older she might have a second career in Oscar Wilde revivals but she would not stoop to play in kitchen sink dramas or any 'new wave' offerings, which was strange considering where she had come from, just a working class girl able to set hearts ablaze with a mere glance from those gorgeous eyes. There would always be men at the stage door and often heavily embossed invitations, sometimes delivered by mysterious means. She had taken all the usual precautions during those stage door liaisons, so she was dismayed when she conceived Victoria and hurt when she had been so callously sloughed off – never heard from the father again, not a word, not a penny either. "So much for noblesse oblige," she had said to herself. And not too long afterwards Roger appeared, complete with gallant proposal.

It was unusual for her to have to seek Roger's advice on anything of much importance, but he had been a good husband and substitute father in his arm's-length way. They had agreed that she would deal with Victoria's upbringing, and he had contributed a series of sensible suggestions at her request when such subjects as schooling arose. She had shown no real interest in his work; in fact she felt rather let down that he was happy as the Curator of the Royal Horological Society, such an ordinary job for a Baronet. Only occasionally had she wondered at Roger's frequent meetings with Hubert. Even if he was Roger's brother, he was, after all, the Commissioner of the Metropolitan Police and their meetings had seldom been social. And she had sometimes felt that the Commissioner's wife had more social entrees than she did.

Roger welcomed her, although a little distractedly. He would never say it, but she realised from his manner that he would have preferred some notice of her arrival. And much to her surprise, he shepherded her into the garden, rather than his Study. They sat under a sun umbrella and she ordered a glass of wine.

"The Tokay Gewurtztraminer, I think," she said to the waiter who walked away shell-shocked by her smile.

Roger was waiting with less patience than usual, so she launched into her plea.

"Roger, I haven't often asked for your help with Victoria, have I?"

He smiled, thinking of all the times he had had to use his ingenuity to plant suggestions when she would have directed Victoria along some unsuitable avenue. It had taken him effort he could ill afford at the time to steer Victoria into the Oxenham College for Ladies.

Antonia ploughed on, "I think she needs some distraction, she has been so withdrawn, not herself at all. Is there anything you could suggest, something in the arts – literature perhaps, you know how good she is at that?"

Roger thought this was one of the more sensible suggestions he could remember, although it was clear that Antonia expected him to open doors into a prestigious appointment that she herself could enjoy.

He was under considerable pressure today; waiting in his Study was a Royal Person, not near the top of the order of succession, but not a person he could ignore for long either.

"Antonia, you know I love Victoria like my own daughter, and I'm honoured that you should ask me to intercede at this difficult time. Let me give it some thought; perhaps tomorrow I can attend to it more fully?"

He got up, signalling that the discussion was at an end.

This angered Antonia. "Really, Roger," she snapped, her eyes blazing, "you can't turn me away like this; I need an answer desperately, I am quite at my wit's end."

Roger heard a line from some melodrama or other, and this pushed him into territory that he rarely allowed himself to visit.

"Antonia, you have come here unannounced at a difficult time for me. I really cannot give you an answer at this very moment. And please understand that to a large extent it is your ambition for Victoria that has created this mess; I could see that she entered into that engagement only to please you. So you must bear with your problem for a few hours longer!"

He walked swiftly away from her. From behind him he could hear a string of words much better left unsaid. Antonia's accent had also slipped. Had Roger been blessed with Jonathan's ear, he might have detected the modified vowels and swallowed consonants that placed her squarely in the rougher parts of the East End of London.

Roger entered his study making his apologies with an unusual abruptness. The Royal Person was clearly not amused, a raised eyebrow appearing on the Royal face.

"Perhaps, Roger, this is not a good time. I'm sure my mother would be interested to know that your other business was more pressing."

This remark did nothing to soothe Roger's hardly contained anger.

He said, forcefully, "Perhaps you will give my humble regards to your most gracious mother, when you next see her?"

He had allowed the slightest stress on the word 'when', indicating his awareness that the Person was not presently in favour with his mother.

There was a tense silence.

The Royal Person finally grinned boyishly. "Never could face you down, could I? Let us move on, shall we? I need some help and, frankly, don't have the foggiest idea where to turn. Left my marker in that new club, side-street near the Dorchester; far too much really, I must have been blotto. Hints that the damned press will be informed if I don't clear it. Quite far outside my ability, frankly."

Roger had previously dealt with similar incidents with good-humoured patience, but was not inclined to do so today. He glared at the person until there was evidence of Royal discomfort.

"How much this time?" he demanded. When he heard the amount, he stood up in fury.

The Person said hastily, "I say, Roger, don't get pious with me! It's only money after all."

"Money you do not have, I take it?"

"Wouldn't be here otherwise."

Sir Roger's exasperation reached boiling point.

"And you think my duties include bailing you out of these stupidities? I advise you to think again. This is what you will do. You will take whatever money you can raise, go to the club and insist on talking to the manager. Offer the money on condition that you see the marker, say you were so drunk you don't remember the amount, or some such excuse. You must see their safe and let me know immediately what make and model it is."

There was a look of outrage on the Royal face.

"You expect me to act like, well, like a damned tradesman? Make and model numbers, no idea what you're talking about."

"Then my resources cannot be made available, not now nor in the future."

Roger had gone out on a limb; whether he would be able to carry it through was another matter.

There was a heavy silence.

"That's it? That's all you will do for me?"

Roger heard the weakness in the Royal voice and smiled grimly.

The Person rose and made for the door, where he turned and drawled, "Haven't exactly polished your image today, Roger, I shall have words to say to certain people."

He left with as much bravado as he could muster.

Roger sat down and ordered a gin and tonic, most unusual for him at this hour.

Jonathan travelled to Oxford on a local train, trying not to think how much depended on winning the Scholarship. Charles' warning about how far the de Quincys might go to harm him weighed heavily. Thank goodness Charles had told him about the red DPS number. He walked up from the station until he saw the grand sign that read 'Abingdon College'. It was all glass and steel, leaving a markedly different impression than the honey-coloured sandstone colleges that went back so many centuries.

The Porter ushered him up some stairs to an anteroom. As was the tradition, the candidates were kept waiting, testing their nerves. There were four of them, three young men and a young woman. Jonathan wore his Chaseman suit, a gift from old Bronsky. It had opened more doors socially and raised more eyebrows than he could recall now; even Travis[17] had been won over by it when Jonathan first arrived at Mountbeck. He had been unable at first to understand the basis for such deference to tailored material, but eventually realised that the perfection of the cut and alignment of the pattern sent a clear signal that the wearer belonged to a particular social class.

The tension in the waiting room was palpable. Jonathan sat behind his stone face, giving nothing away, but nervous nonetheless. One of the two other young men was bantering with anyone who would listen, his voice plummy and affected, his tie announcing his attendance at one of England's two top schools. Jonathan thought it was easier to put on a tie than a suit; in either case it didn't necessarily mean a thing. He had put on the tie that he had been lent by the de Quincys when he had first gone to see Victoria at Frodsham. He had no idea what it represented.

On the other side of the room, the young woman had crossed a promising pair of legs and was swinging the free one. The movement, possibly by design, was a constant distraction. He recalled the book on camouflage: 'of all the causes of breakdown in concealment, the one to avoid is movement'. He had absorbed the entire book and anything else the College library had on the subject. The article on the chameleon and its apparent ability to blend into any background had particularly fascinated him. It had come as a disappointment that this was a myth; chameleons change colour but not in response to their background. The other young man appeared to be less concerned than the rest of them. He was writing answers into the *Times* crossword, his gold pen flashing non-stop. Eventually he threw the newspaper aside in disdain, as though it was beneath his intellectual capacity.

---

17   Travis is the Butler at Mountbeck.

The secretary entered and called the banterer in first. He emerged a few minutes later with a smug smile on his face as though to say, "Give up, you people, I'm the chosen one!"

The crossword genius was invited in next and lasted somewhat longer. Jonathan picked up the copy of the *Times* and was amused to see that the letters entered so confidently and swiftly were nonsense, random letters inserted purely for effect. He laughed, and on a whim handed the paper to the young woman, saying, "Nice trick, but needs more stagecraft."

She hardly glanced at it, and he noticed that her knuckles were white with suppressed anxiety. She bit her lip and didn't respond.

When she was called, she sat for a moment, almost traumatised. The secretary encouraged her to go forward. A few minutes later she emerged with the secretary helping her, a handkerchief pressed to her mouth. They left the room. When the secretary returned, she said, "Poor girl, quite overcome, I hope she will recover."

She invited Jonathan to follow her. As the door closed, she announced, "Mr. Hare, gentlemen," and took her place off to the side.

Jonathan was faced with a refectory table at which five men were seated. A picture window was behind the table and he was looking directly into the light. In a far corner of the room and somewhat in the shadows, another older man was seated. There was no chair for Jonathan. He looked around and spotted a folding chair leaning against a far wall. He walked over and snapped it open, placing it so that he could look at the men without the light in his eyes. "May I sit here?" he asked.

There was a silence while glances were exchanged. Some notes were made.

The man in the middle of the table opened the interview. Perhaps this is the Master, thought Jonathan. There had been no introductions.

"You know why we have invited you here today, I take it?"

"Yes, sir, it's to decide whether I am worthy of the Galdraith Scholarship."

This seemed to satisfy the men.

"Ah yes, Jonathan Hare, isn't it? Excellent results at 'A' levels. Doctor Harris has a few questions about your mathematics results."

A man leaned forward. He had a thin face and unruly hair and was wearing a disreputable tweed jacket with leather patches at the elbows.

"To tell you the truth, Hare," he grated, "I can't see how you could have answered all the questions in the time allotted, unless you had most improper knowledge of the paper beforehand. After all, you only needed to answer five of the ten."

There was something about the man that Jonathan found offensive. He tried his best to keep his temper.

"Doctor Harris, there are two things I would like to say. First, the examination instructions said 'full marks may be obtained for complete answers to five questions; partial answers obtain fewer marks'. That isn't quite the same as 'answer five questions only'."

There were sounds of feet shuffling and Jonathan could swear he heard the man in the corner choke back a laugh. When he looked over there he was surprised to see that it was Lord Galdraith himself. The photograph the librarian had given him was a good likeness, not flattering certainly.

Doctor Harris cleared his throat. "I stand corrected. But you said you had two things to say?"

Jonathan thought how to express this without giving offence. "I believe you last set the Joint Oxford and Cambridge Mathematics paper three years ago, and I noticed that three years seems to be a common cycle. So I worked on all your past papers and read all your books. Your interests naturally turned up in this paper."

There was some clearing of throats at the table.

Doctor Harris was not finished. "So will you take the same approach here at University?" Jonathan smiled, "Only if the university uses the same examination method."

There was some discomfort at the table. The Master seemed the most annoyed.

"This isn't a game, Hare, we are a renowned university and students graduating from here may expect to be held in the highest regard. I find your last answer to Doctor Harris to be unsavoury."

Jonathan shrugged, which irritated the panel. The Master opened a file and scanned the contents.

"You understand that the Galdraith Scholar must be above reproach and comport himself with dignity. Any cheap tricks such as you have employed will not do. Simply will not do. I shall ask our Proctor to deal with the next subject."

A burly man, looking much like an ex-policeman, looked sharply at Jonathan. "You claim in your application to have no criminal record?"

Jonathan, aware of the hostility now in the room, answered politely, "That is correct, sir."

"And you would agree that the Scholarship could not be awarded to anyone so convicted?"

"Of course," Jonathan said, perhaps a bit sarcastically.

"Then perhaps you could explain this?"

He pushed a document in Jonathan's direction distastefully. The other members had their files already open.

Jonathan had a premonition that all was not well. The document started:

Metropolitan Police – Statement of Offences
Subject – Jonathan Hare alias Samuel Ward

He pretended to read the document, a cold sweat starting.

So they had used it after all and at the cruellest time. Don't panic, he thought, you know what Charles told you.

He looked up at the Proctor. "May I assume that you have experience with these documents, sir?"

The Master interceded, "You are here to answer our questions, not conduct a cross-examination!"

Jonathan stared at the Master. "But, sir, this document is a fake. I believe that with the Proctor's help I can show that."

There was consternation at the table. Jonathan heard the words 'disgraceful' and 'want no part of it'.

Eventually the Master nodded to the Proctor, who glared at Jonathan. "Yes, Mr. Hare, I do have such experience."

Jonathan took a moment to decide on his next words. The tension in the room was almost overpowering.

"It doesn't have a DPS number in the top right hand corner so it can't be official."

The Master had gone white. The Proctor was spluttering with rage.

Jonathan suddenly felt overwhelmed; the thought that the de Quincys would go this far to discredit him made him want to vomit. He stood up and said, "Excuse me," and hurried out of the room. Behind him he heard raised voices from the other room.

He found a lavatory and washed his face and took several deep breaths. He went back to the anteroom and was picking up his hat when the secretary rushed in.

"Oh, please Mr. Hare, don't leave. Lord Galdraith wishes to speak with you."

When he hesitated, she said, "I think you would be wise to listen to him."

And to his surprise, she was blushing.

FIVE

Out of the Miry Clay

WHEN JONATHAN RETURNED TO THE ROOM, EVERYONE had left except Lord Galdraith and the Master. The Master escorted Jonathan to Lord Galdraith and introduced him.

"You already knew who I was, didn't you?" asked Lord Galdraith with a friendly smile. Jonathan heard those long rounded vowels and the deliberate cadence that people use around Oxford and along the Thames. He felt comfortable with the accent; it had no affectation about it, signalling that the speaker was not interested in identifying high, or for that matter, low class people by their manner of speech. He felt a little better.

The Master cleared his throat. "It would appear, Mr. Hare, that apologies are called for. I trust you will understand that the members were misled by that document. I have charged the Proctor with a formal investigation to discover how such a mistake was made."

He looked at Lord Galdraith for approval.

Lord Galdraith had risen to his position of wealth and influence partly because he was adept at judging people and selecting them with care. He had once heard a military expression: 'time spent in reconnaissance is never wasted' – and had been guided by it as his empire grew.

"So, Mr. Hare, let me see if I have got this right. You spent time and effort understanding the university methods for setting exams and noted that certain specialized questions appeared at regular intervals. Then you associated the subjects with the author, Doctor Harris, and decided that this year's 'A' level exam would be set by him, giving you a decided advantage. Clearly, the distinction awarded you was no mistake!"

Jonathan was about to confirm this when Lord Galdraith continued. "And you had gone to the trouble of finding out some background on me, including a photograph, I take it?"

Jonathan agreed.

Lord Galdraith turned to the Master, "Sounds like a research candidate to me!"

The Master's face was a bit flushed, thought Jonathan.

"Well, what else did you find out?" asked Lord Galdraith.

Jonathan felt more accepted by the industrialist than anyone in a long time. He edited the librarian's material as he went.

"Your Lordship was awarded the Peerage in the New Year's Honours list two years ago. Most people assumed that it was for your generosity in founding this College. You built a manufacturing empire and sustained it through difficult times both before and after the war and held the majority of shares privately."

He paused and looked quickly at Lord Galdraith, who said, "Don't stop now, man!"

"I believe your wife died a year ago, sir, after a long illness."

There was a silence.

Lord Galdraith cleared his throat, "Children?"

Jonathan had to think. "Son named Frederic; daughter, much younger, named after your wife, sir, Hilary, I think."

By now, the industrialist had a triumphant smile.

"There, Howard," he said to the Master, "How about that for research? I told you I'd be right – instincts, you know."

He got up and shook Jonathan's hand. "Congratulations, Mr. Hare, the Scholarship is yours. And now I want you to meet my daughter."

He went to the door and brought in the young woman with the promising legs. Jonathan stared, but managed to get his stone face in place.

"This is our first Scholar, my dear; his name is Jonathan Hare. This is my daughter Hilary."

Any young man emerging from an all-male boarding school education has learned the essential art of concealing his feelings so Jonathan was able to disguise his surprise. He shook Hilary's hand and said, "An excellent piece of stagecraft; fooled me completely; I thought you had expired from nerves!"

Hilary blushed, "It was my father's idea; he wanted to test them all, but I could see that you were the one to focus on, those other two, ewh!"

From which Jonathan gathered that she thought they were beneath consideration.

Lord Galdraith was watching this interchange.

"We do this all the time for top management interviews, set up some sort of trauma to jack up the tension; it sorts out the men from the boys! But you will want to see your Rooms, Mr. Hare; perhaps Hilary will show you them while we finish up here."

Jonathan and Hilary went down the stairs and across the interior quadrangle. She was nearly as tall as him and pleasant to look at, but it was her bearing that caught his attention. She was willowy and moved with a straight back and airy lightness.

"Ballet lessons, I bet!" he said to himself.

She became aware of him watching the swing of her hips and her graceful stride. She smiled, "A girl has to work so hard these days!"

Jonathan was mystified and tried, "You make it seem effortless."

She stopped and faced him, "You're good, Jonathan Hare, you're good!"

He had no idea what she meant. They reached a staircase and she led the way, apparently unconscious of the additional length of leg that she was displaying. Jonathan hoped the staircase was a long one, but all too soon they reached a door that she unlocked. On the door was a plaque that announced 'Galdraith Scholar'; beneath it was a slot for the Scholar's name.

The Rooms came with every amenity, however plain and functional. Jonathan was having difficulty containing his joy; it was the sort of place he had dreamed of all his life; it even had a telephone. Someone must have pulled strings to get that. It had nothing of the shabby utility furnishings like those at home, or of the heavy Victorian fussiness of the room at Mountbeck. Someone with a modern taste had chosen the décor. He walked around the living room touching everything and investigating the appliances. He went through a door into a bedroom furnished in a warm and surprisingly welcoming style. It felt a little too cosy to him, the word 'boudoir' swimming into his mind. There were one or two touches that might better suit a girl, he thought.

It dawned on him that Hilary's presence might not be coincidental. He returned to the living room to find her standing at the window. The light was streaming in and outlining her figure through her white blouse. She may be slender, he thought, but she is very nicely shaped. She turned from the window with a smile, "Did you like what you saw?"

He was stumped; whatever did she mean? She might still be testing him; after all, what a wonderful job she had done putting on that anxiety and trauma in the anteroom. He found that he was enjoying the challenge, and decided to join in the fun.

"Everything I've seen so far is just perfect." He managed to keep his face straight.

She raised an eyebrow, "So far, Jonathan?"

He felt the ground moving beneath his feet; somehow he couldn't resist taking the next step. "You mean there is more to see?"

She burst into laughter, "I did say you were good, Jonathan, but you mustn't get cheeky!"

He grinned at her, still not entirely sure what she meant.

He decided to play another card. "Did you think that the first Scholar might be a girl, Hilary?"

She looked startled. "Why do you ask?"

He sensed that he might be entering dangerous territory, but pushed on regardless. "The bedroom would suit a girl just as well as a man."

There was a silence. She was blushing. Suddenly she spun away from him, high on her toes, her arms floating outwards. She travelled a few feet, her skirts flaring, and stopped. She turned to him. "Do you recognize that?"

He was lost once more, but had developed some momentum. "Ballet steps, ballerina escaping from a trap, perhaps?"

She put her hands on her hips and frowned at him. "And I thought I had you pegged," she said. From which he decided she was playing a game of one-upmanship.

"We only met today, Hilary," he said, "I may not be as easily 'pegged' as that."

She was staring at him; he was quite sure she was going to continue the verbal jousting. He thought they were equal on points.

Instead, she nodded towards the bedroom. "Show me what you mean, then."

They went in together and, taking her interest at face value, he pointed out the flowery curtains and fringed cushions.

"The padded headboard doesn't exactly fit my idea of a man's room, either!"

She was behind him, and, when he turned, she had closed the door and was leaning against it.

When she spoke, her voice had changed. "Does it make you uncomfortable, Jonathan?"

He thought they had resumed the jousting. "I could get used to it, I think."

"Well then," she said and pushed him onto the bed, "so could I!"

William Jason had so looked forward to his job as Head Porter at Galdraith College that he spent most of his time there, even though it was a couple of weeks before the start of the Michaelmas Term. He had noted Miss Hilary showing the young man up to the Scholar's Rooms. He assumed that this must be the Scholar, since the interview was scheduled for today, and he had been tasked with setting up the Master's Study. He had thought it was a bit of sharp practice making the candidates squint into the light, but the Master had insisted.

He was holding a letter addressed to a Mr. Jonathan Hare, Galdraith Interview, Abingdon College. The envelope was expensive and the family crest was impressive. Since his duties included overseeing the preparation of the Scholar's Rooms, he took the letter, marched up the stairs and knocked with military precision on the door.

Hilary had fallen on Jonathan and kissed him with such abandon that when they heard the knocking they were both a bit stunned. She jumped off the bed laughing hysterically. She ought not to be laughing like that, he thought; he hadn't seen this coming, and he felt affronted that she had taken the initiative. Anyway, he thought, surely she wasn't that desperate that she would want to seduce him an hour after they had met?

She was hastily smoothing down her skirt. "Saved by the bell, this round anyway! Come on, we had better go into the other room."

She took his hand for a moment, pulled him into the living room and opened the door.

"Oh, Jason, thank you for coming, there are one or two changes that Mr. Hare would like. Can you put back the plain headboard? The padded one is too fancy after all. And this is Mr. Jonathan Hare, the Galdraith Scholar."

Jonathan shook Jason's hand. The grip was strong and he noticed that the man held himself rigidly upright. He was reminded of newspaper pictures of the famous Regimental Sergeant Major in the Grenadier Guards, the man with the loudest voice in England, according to the blurb.

"Were you in the Army, Mr. Jason?" he tried.

Jason swelled with pride, "Coldstream Guards, sir, finest regiment on the face of the earth! Stay there all my life if they'd let me. Not that I don't enjoy this appointment, Miss Hilary," he added hastily.

She laughed, "And a wonderful piece of luck for the College that we could get you, Jason." Jonathan stored this information away.

She told Jason that she would be bringing some replacement curtains and cushions. "You were right, after all, Jason," she laughed. "A bit too feminine for such masculine tastes."

Jason stood a bit taller. "Never let a word pass my lips, Miss."

"You didn't need to; your face said it all."

Jason looked at Jonathan. "Better watch out for Miss Hilary, sir, she's a quick one!"

Jonathan thought that was a bit too near the truth.

"Oh, there is this letter for you, sir, looked important. Clever of them to put this address on it," said Jason, taking his leave.

Hilary was looking at the letter in Jonathan's hand. Her attitude had changed perceptibly.

"You can move in any time you like, just let Jason know you're coming. He keeps all the keys, just in case."

She moved to the door and said, "You were right, Jonathan, I don't have you pegged at all."

And then she had gone, leaving him speechless and even more convinced that he'd never get the hang of these strange creatures called women.

Alone in his Rooms, he savoured the moment. He had a place of his own at last, well, for as long as he was the Scholar. For most of his life he had been housed in anonymous school dormitories and shared a Common Room with a host of others, most of whom didn't share his tastes or views. He did have his room at home, but he was so seldom there.

Out of the blue a cold sweat started; the memory of that document at the interview had returned. What did they hope to gain? They clearly didn't want him to win the Scholarship. It couldn't be that he was a threat to them, surely?

He had done nothing to deserve such treatment; in fact he had helped to catch that Gang. There had been a lot of press coverage and guess who took the credit? The Commissioner, of course! So why would they attack him? He scratched his head; at least he was safe from Arthur

Salmon. But the more he thought about it the more difficulty he had recalling Arthur's name among the arrested. He shrugged; surely the police couldn't have missed Arthur? And now that he was the Galdraith Scholar, the de Quincys wouldn't attack him again, would they? He felt a little better; now he ought to focus on getting a First[18], then he would be set for life, he thought.

But lurking behind this determined focus on his academic future was a sense of insecurity; he had made enemies and they might choose to attack him again.

---

18   A First Class Honours Degree, essential for an academic career at the major Universities.

Six

The Fallout

REGINALD FORSYTH, PROCTOR OF GALDRAITH COLLEGE, was sitting in his study in a black temper. He was aware that it was his police experience that had been the deciding factor in his appointment. Perhaps the Master hadn't fully realised that a senior policeman never really leaves the service; they carry with them case knowledge that may be needed in the future. So when that telephone call came from the very top of the system and more or less ordered him to confront the Hare person with the Statement of Offences he'd jumped at the chance. He had eventually realised that the document was not authentic, but it would take a procedural expert to spot that, he had been sure. Quite how Hare had this knowledge was a question he would pursue later. Meanwhile, he had the delicate job of finding some explanation for the Master, and even worse, reporting the failure of the strategy to the top brass.

Lord Galdraith and the Master had signed various documents that put the official stamp on Jonathan's appointment. Lord Galdraith was feeling pleased with himself, for he had taken a liking to Hare, and had been impressed with how he had handled himself at the interview.

"Wiped the floor with that bumped-up schoolmaster Harris," he said to himself.

At the back of his mind, however, there lurked a strange feeling surrounding the matter of the police document. He hadn't really grasped the implications and Hare had disposed of it in such a comprehensive manner that his attention had been caught more by Hare's body language than the contents of the document. There arose in his mind the notion that Hare had somehow expected the thing to happen, been prepared for it even. He cleared his throat.

"What was all that about, the Proctor's document I mean, a bit cloak and dagger wasn't it?"

The Master had his own apprehensions. "I really don't understand it; if it wasn't genuine, and I'm sure it could not have been, otherwise the Proctor wouldn't have been so easily stumped, what on earth was the purpose? If Hare had no explanation, had floundered, even, we would have had to dismiss him, even report him to the local police."

There was a silence while the men worked out that, if Jonathan had indeed been a fugitive, the Proctor would have had police waiting to arrest him.

The Master shook his head. "I promise you, William, that I'll get to the bottom of it. Let's hope it was just some bureaucratic bungling; lots more of that around these days, no sense of vocation in the Civil Service, just a bunch of trade unionists, if you ask me."

He said this in part to please Lord Galdraith, whose antipathy to the Labour movement was well-known.

On her way back across the quadrangle, Hilary was scolding herself for her stupidity. She had badly misjudged Jonathan, although there had been nothing in his application to indicate what sort of young man he might be. She knew that he was the favoured candidate; his exam results had put him in a rare class and she had understood that idiot Harris's resistance, for Jonathan had made the exam that he had set look childish. She suspected that Jonathan would have suffered at the interview simply because of that.

She had known immediately when Jonathan noticed her in the ante-room, and had allowed him a generous view of her legs, which she knew were always attracting men's attention, sometimes welcome, sometimes not. He had signalled his interest by passing over that crossword – as though she would know anything about such juvenile pastimes!

She had felt that she had done a good job of the nervous breakdown, but he had said, 'excellent stagecraft', as if he knew all about it. She threw her mind back to the crossword incident; hadn't he used the same words then, 'needs more stagecraft'? She nodded to herself. She had missed both signals at the time, had been so pleased with her perform-ance that she hadn't allowed for the fact that he had seen through it all. He had been very polite about it, hadn't he, crafty bugger, teasing her all the time, she thought, blushing with embarrassment.

She remembered sensing that he was admiring her as they walked across the quad; she hadn't been trying really, but she had been pleased by his increased interest. Going up the stairs first had been a bit brazen, but all part of the game. By the time they had started looking around the room, she had decided to try him out. And how he had responded! So smooth, all the right words, she couldn't best him, try as she might. And he had so neatly manoeuvred them into the bedroom; she had panicked for a moment, thinking he was a Lothario in sheep's clothing. She smiled grimly at the mixed metaphor. By the time they were in there, well, she was getting excited, wasn't she? Couldn't blame her for taking the first step, surely? And what might have happened had Jason not arrived at the vital moment? She had managed the untimely arrival rather well, she thought, and hoped she hadn't babbled about the change of décor; it was the only thing she could think of at the time.

But what had upset her most was the letter. What on earth was he doing with a letter like that, with the family crest so obvious? She wondered how she could have been so far off with her assessment. She stopped in shock at the bottom of the stairs to the Master's Study. Jonathan had been wearing a suit with such a superb cut! She had picked him beforehand as the best candidate and the suit had simply been part of her image of what he ought to look like. And that tie, well, what a subtlety, wearing an old Balliol tie to an interview at a new College, it must have caused some raised eyebrows! She was so unsettled that it took her the climb up to the Study before the next image came at her; Jason had called him 'sir' as soon as Jonathan had spoken to him. What on earth did that signify? Jason, that terror of cadets at Sandhurst, that upright and proud veteran of the War, was a holder of some big medal, she remembered. Yet he hadn't hesitated to acknowledge Jonathan as someone worthy of that simple accolade – 'sir'.

The Royal family tree is like a giant Sherwood oak; all the power appears at first to be in the main trunk. There are scores of small branches created by secondary offspring, none of them in the line of succession. Queen Victoria's children and their children account for a small army of noble and influential people. But lineage is not necessarily the criterion for power; some high in succession were content to escape the overpowering treadmill of duties, hardly ever in the press unless some scandal could be dug up, while others perhaps only on the periphery had become wielders of immense influence.

The Royal Person's mother dominated the power brokers. Her house in Eaton Square, outstanding even in that aristocratic oasis, received a steady stream of shadowy figures, either summoned, in which case the speed of their response was legendary, or by social invitation. Prime Ministers would sometimes serve an entire term without crossing her doorstep, while others might come to know her well. It was generally agreed that the saying 'to know her is to love her' did not necessarily apply; in fact, those in the know referred to her, but never in her presence, as 'Lady Hecate'[19].

Her greatest sorrow was that with all her power and influence she did not have a son of whom she could be proud. Quite the contrary, he had been a constant source of shame and had frittered away a lot of her energy that she could have used elsewhere to greater effect. And now he had really gone beyond the limit. She decided it was time to put her foot

---

19   Hecate is the goddess of witchcraft and sorcery.

down, and, as was her habit, immediately picked up the telephone and summoned her son to Eaton Square.

When he arrived, Rutherford, her man-servant, announced him with a chill in his voice that perhaps only she could hear.

She waved him into a chair just far enough away to avoid any sense of intimacy.

"I understand that you are, once more, in financial trouble."

It was said without pity or understanding.

She watched him squirm, but he knew better than to prevaricate.

"Yes, mother, I've signed a note at a club in Mayfair, a new one. I can't honour it, I'm afraid. I have asked Roger de Quincy to help, but he wasn't very kind – made me go and do his dirty work for him."

She heard him shuffling off responsibility as usual; it was Roger who was supposed to get him out of another hole of his own making.

She let him stew, hoping he would at last understand that he must accept the consequences of his behaviour.

But he took her silence as acceptance of his story.

"People at the Club are being quite horrid, Mother, talking about 'actions'. I don't understand it; the other places didn't make such a fuss, glad to have me, what?"

She refused to respond.

"Hope it doesn't get into the papers; it would do us no good at all."

She heard his easy manipulation at work; perhaps she had been weak in the past, she thought, in allowing him to shift the blame. It was now the family's good name that he was trying to hide behind.

Lady Hecate made a decision that she might have made many years ago; she turned her haughtiest face to her son and said, "I shall rely on Sir Roger to give you as much assistance as he can."

She stood up, signalling that the interview was at an end. Her son stumbled to his feet, stammering, "What am I to do?"

Rutherford, aware as always of the perfect time to intercede, came in and shepherded him from the room.

Jonathan was sitting in a low and comfortable chair, running over the events of the day. He was tired, he realised, not healthy-tired like after a good fast bike ride, but with that drawn feeling behind the eyes that he had experienced after the all-night adventure in Arthur's warehouse, trying to get Jane out of there. He couldn't help wondering how just a few years could make the difference between Jane's innocent admiration of him and Hilary's rather alarming sexual aggressiveness. What might have happened if Jason hadn't come knocking?

He remembered that Charmaine[20] had kissed him while they were dancing. Now *that* was a kiss; he had felt he was going to faint with the excitement. But Charmaine had been so much older, six or seven years at least, maybe more. What did he know? He hadn't gone there with any idea that she would come on to him that way. Before anything could happen, she had broken it off and sent him away. What had she said? "Who are you?" as though he had done something to frighten her. He shrugged, thinking it was all too complicated.

He was holding the letter in the blue envelope; he had known immediately that it was from Victoria. His anxiety returned; Sir Roger was her father and Jonathan was sure that it had been him who had persuaded Edward to dismiss him that night at Mountbeck. Edward wouldn't have done that without the sort of pressure that Sir Roger could apply. But that wasn't Victoria's fault; she didn't have a clue what her father really did. When he had last seen her at the Society after the escape from the warehouse, far across the room and shielded by her mother, she had looked quite awful. She'd had black bags under her eyes and her hair was dragged back in an unflattering style. He opened the letter, and read:

---

20 An undercover police agent tasked with keeping an eye on Jonathan when he was in London. He knew her as a dancing instructress.

Dear Jonathan,

I am sorry we weren't able to talk when you were at the Society, but that Jane Bellestream so monopolized you and my mother always seemed to be in the way.

You never told me where you lived but I remembered my father talking about the Interview, so I thought this might reach you. I hope so.

As you can see I am back at Frodsham. Please, Jonathan, would you telephone me when you have a moment, it would mean a lot to me.

Your friend,

Victoria.

He read the letter again, torn between his fear of the far-reaching influence of the de Quincy brothers and a sudden curiosity about Victoria's situation that took him by surprise. He had no idea of the social significance of Victoria's engagement, but he remembered how much Lady Antonia had relished telling him about it in the car when he went back to London that time. She had intended it cruelly to make quite sure that he knew not to approach Victoria again. He had fended off that barb, pretending a lack of interest; Lady Antonia had left the car with barely concealed annoyance.

But Victoria had not only broken off the engagement, she had sent him that clipping from the *Tatler*. He realised that he had no comprehension of Victoria's situation, in fact, he thought, he had almost no knowledge of girls of his own age. Seven years in boarding schools had hardly prepared him for sensible relationships with young women. He had no sisters, and his mother had made it clear that she would be displeased if he wasted his time on the local girls.

He had been fifteen when he and Victoria had met and begun a short friendship, well, he thought, more like pen pals really. His mother had never found out about Victoria and it hadn't lasted long; Victoria's mother had seen to that.

He had run into Victoria a couple of times when he was in London, and he supposed they had remained friends.

He propped the letter on the mantelpiece. He didn't need to decide anything today, did he?

The Royal Person telephoned Sir Roger.

"Did your dirty work, Roger; had to insist, but got to see the safe. All I can tell you is that it has 'Champion' on the door. Couldn't see anything else, no numbers; didn't want to be too obvious about it, of course."

Sir Roger thought that was par for the course; the man was a waste of time. He sat back and felt slightly ill. Of all the safes, it just had to be a Champion. Perhaps Harry Sparrow could advise him. Harry knew his way around; there must be a mechanic somewhere that could open it; got to get that marker back; far too much damage if the story gets into the Press.

He had another thought; he would delegate this to Colin Davies, make him work for his promotion to Inspector. He had earned it, the way he stepped in and rescued Jane Bellestream and Jon – no Hare, he corrected himself. And Colin had no idea of the disaster surrounding the plan to discredit Hare, so he'd be on better terms with the lad.

He had pushed Jonathan as far out of his mind as he was able. The fellow was far too dangerous; he simply knew too much, and had worked out the details of their operation, even slipped in a blow beneath the belt, what was it? Something like 'whoever had arranged the kidnapping ought to pay the price'.

He and Hubert had both been at high risk; he'd had no misgivings about the plan in the beginning, and the end clearly justified the means. But conspiring to kidnap an aristocrat, well, it would finish both of them.

And then there had been Victoria. He had grown to love her almost in spite of Antonia. What a disaster with that fool Robert; the damned man had other options; it was not done to impregnate a servant and abandon her. The fact that Robert hadn't made proper arrangements spoke volumes. He was proud of Victoria's rebellion, and surprised that she had withstood all of Antonia's dramatics.

There was something else, though, something to do with Hare; he recalled the incident in the garden. She had insisted that he send Hare out as soon as he had finished the interview. He had wondered at her heightened animation, unusual for her; she seemed almost desperate to talk to the lad. What had she said? 'Least you can do, father; making me identify him like that, I feel like a traitor.'

He had watched them until they had gone down the rhododendron walk; there was something between them, certainly more than casual acquaintance. Damned Hare fellow, always complicating things.

He realised this was childish; given other circumstances he would be glad to have him as part of the Service.

Inspector Colin Davies had a high regard for Jonathan Hare. What was the lad – seventeen? – but he had fully earned a degree of respect. Martin, the de Quincys' factotum, seemed to have a soft spot for him too, and the staff at Mountbeck had certainly been won over. And yet, thought Colin, the young man didn't go out of his way to impress; he just had that air about him. Girls were attracted to him too, but he seemed unaware of it.

Colin recalled being invited for tea in the Mountbeck kitchens, and how Daisy had expressed what she would like to do with the lad; it had taken them by surprise, hadn't it? It would have been all right coming from a Cockney floozy, but it was somehow even more picturesque when someone so far from the Smoke used those words. Mrs. White pretending to be shocked, it was a bit of a laugh, really!

Being a minder for Jonathan at Mountbeck had been a bonus holiday; he had to keep an eye open, but nothing much happened. Sir Roger had briefed him well, so he had known that Harry had pulled a similar duty for the Bessemer people, staying at the 'Station Hotel' in Thirsk, he recalled. But Harry had seemed disinterested, certainly only did a small amount of fieldwork. Daisy's mum had served him in the village pub and recognised the photo right away.

Travis had commented on how hard Mr. Hare had worked at making Lady Jane his friend, apparently because that French girl, Germaine, had begged him to. Travis suggested that if he ever succeeded it would be some sort of miracle; the young girl was hopeless at relationships, still traumatized after losing all her family.

The Inspector decided to telephone Travis and was surprised by how icily the butler responded. It didn't matter what he said, Travis was not going to divulge where the lad could be found.

Harry Sparrow was lonely. He had hit all his local haunts, trying to enjoy the liveliness of the 'King's Head' – he recalled Jonathan's reaction when he and Rita had called it the 'Loaf of Bread', or simply 'Loaf'; it must have been difficult for him, all that Cockney slang. That prompted the first laugh he had had for days. Jonathan had so quickly adopted the Cockney accent that he had been able to fool Sergeant Colin Davies, and that wouldn't have been easy. Harry and Colin had become – what would you call it? – not friends exactly; perhaps they just understood each other, each useful to the other, a world of contacts between them, with many of them operating in the shadows, like him really.

After a while, he realised that when he thought of the woman who had shared his house, he thought of her as 'Rita'. He had worked out, eventually, that she was a plant, and not just from the Bessemer people; he had known about that, she had been quite open about it, hadn't she?

She had pulled some really deep scam, he wasn't sure exactly what, but had given her real name away doing it – Annabel Winstanley – aunt living somewhere near Mountbeck, must be, the scam wouldn't have worked otherwise. It accounted for some of her clothes and visits to Harrods; he hadn't thought much about that at the time, a mistake, really. She wasn't bad looking, but, boy, had she ever kept him at arm's-length; not that he fancied her, just a bit strange to have a woman in the house, supposed to be his girl, and nothing!

The telephone rang. To his surprise, and with a surge of pleasure, he heard Colin Davies at the other end. They chatted easily for a while, and then Colin said, "We need to talk, Harry, not local either, any suggestions?"

Harry remembered that Colin liked a glass of wine. "There's a wine cellar, south of Holborn, right under the railway viaduct; lawyers like it, won't see any of our types in there!"

Inspector Davies, enjoying his boost in pay, thought this was an excellent idea, not too far on the train, either. They agreed that they could make it by lunchtime.

Harry was nursing a Guinness, none of that frog stuff for him, and Colin was savouring a Moselle something or other – sounded like medicine to Harry, what with the word 'Doktor' on the label.

Colin told Harry about the promotion. Harry had a hard time restraining himself and pumped Colin's hand, saying, "Do I have to call you 'sir' now?"

They laughed.

Harry lowered his voice, not that anyone would have heard, all them suits and wing collars blabbing away, the place packed, they were lucky to get in, weren't they?

"Still a black boy, then?"

By this Harry meant a member of Special Branch or some such, Harry had never been quite sure. Colin simply nodded.

They got down to business. The Inspector, conscious that Sir Roger expected performance for promotion, told Harry, "There's a Champion safe in a club in Mayfair, needs to be eased, something has to be removed, very important."

And important to me, too, he thought.

Harry's face had changed. "Are you serious? I wouldn't touch that with a ten foot pole; Champions are too dangerous for the likes of me and me mates."

Harry had grown to like Jonathan, for all his snotty ways, like he wouldn't answer to any nicknames, just 'Jonathan'; he wouldn't eat in cheap caffs[21], and he wore a toff's[22] suit. Still he was the best safe easer Harry had ever met; he had a sixth sense, hadn't he?

Colin sucked his teeth. He had been afraid Harry would say that. He raised an eyebrow.

Harry knew it wasn't fair, but he lashed out at Colin, "That bloody boss of yours; he set the lad up, really marked his ticket, put him in harm's way, then dropped him like a stone!"

Colin was shocked that Harry had worked out his relationship to Sir Roger. He couldn't believe that Sir Roger was guilty of such treachery.

"What are you on about, Harry?"

Harry wondered how far he should go; some of what he suspected he had worked out while mooning about at home.

"I think they used Jonathan as bait, knew Arthur was after him, got Arthur to send Sailor to pick him up; lovely scam, nearly fooled me and I was listening in. Only thing was that young girl, Jane something, got involved, not sure how. They thought Sailor would take Jonathan and lead them to Arthur, probably some sort of big show, round up the whole Gang."

Colin hadn't drunk any more of his wine because Harry's account was so different from what he had been told.

He had to find some cover. "Could have shown them where to find Arthur anytime, couldn't we, Harry!"

Harry nodded. "But not the patch bosses as well."

Harry thought he had said enough; he had managed to keep Rita out of it, hadn't he?

Colin Davies sat silently for a while. What Harry couldn't have known was how Jonathan, as well as getting Lady Jane out of there, had been able to convince Sailor to rat on Arthur. Used some sort of paper from the safe that proved that Arthur was gypping the Gang, bank accounts in

---

21 A 'caff' is a cheap eating place, short for cafeteria.
22 A 'toff' is any person of much higher class – an abbreviation for 'toffee-nosed', itself indicating an attitude of superiority.

some place in South America, 'San' something or other,[23] it was a pity he hadn't taken a copy; it might have been useful if this went wrong.

But he still had the problem of the safe in Mayfair.

"Where is Mr. Hare now, Harry?"

Harry glared at the Inspector. "Oh, it's *Mr*. Hare now, is it?"

"Look, Harry, I can see why you're upset, but don't take it out on me. Whatever we call him, in my book he's the real hero, deserves most of the credit, behaved properly; what did Lady Jane call him? 'Knight in shining armour'. So, he may be young, but he deserves respect."

Harry wasn't going to be moved. "You tell that boss of yours he's crapped in his own corner; don't ask me to put Jonathan in harm's way, I won't do it!"

Colin knew Harry well enough to accept that, at least for now, he wasn't going to get anywhere. But what would he say to Sir Roger?

Sir Roger had been told the news of the debacle at the Galdraith interview. At first he railed at the incompetence of others; it seemed that he had to do everything himself, and then he began to ponder the possible consequences. How on earth had Hare repulsed the attack? It should have put him out of the race, at least.

Now that the fellow had the protection of 'he Galdraith people, he was an even bigger threat. And he would have money too, not a lot, perhaps, but less susceptible to the usual manipulation. Then he recalled his cavalier promise to Jonathan of additional money as a retainer; even hinted at a bank account in Oxford, regular payments, all that. But the marker problem remained and Colin had not got anywhere with Harry Sparrow; even reported Harry's words, some vulgarity about having sullied my own quarters, or words to that effect.

He told himself that he was starting to get paranoid about Hare, but ever since he and Hubert had decided to sacrifice him for the greater good, things had gone wrong; first that young Jane Bellestream got in

---

23   It was actually a Bearer Bond drawn on a Bank in San Marino that Jonathan
      had removed from Arthur's safe.

the way then Hare somehow got out of the warehouse so early, nearly brought the whole plan to a halt. He wasn't sure what had happened next. According to Colin, Hare had found a way to get the Gang's plan out of Sailor Wilson, but he doubted that. Why would Hare put himself in harm's way if he knew what he and Hubert had done to him? He was sure that the young man had worked that out, otherwise why that sinister remark about 'those responsible having to pay the price'?

He had a splitting headache; unusual for him, he realised.

Jonathan went home to get his belongings, happy with winning the Scholarship and having modern rooms of his own. But he'd have to keep his concerns away from his mother; if he told her about his enemies she would feel obliged to intervene and what a disaster that would be. So when he got there, he hugged her and said, "Good news, mother, I got the Scholarship and it comes with rooms, everything new, I even have a telephone."

He was oblivious to the look of dismay on her face.

His mother was taken aback when he hugged her and more so by the news that he would reside in College. She had assumed that he would live at home, just a short train ride to Oxford, after all.

But she knew him well; he would want his independence and she had become used to his absence, with all those years at boarding school. And she had missed him this summer; what he was doing in London was none of her business, she supposed, and he hadn't told her much. "Just work, mother!" was about the size of it.

What a life she had had, one mistake and the family abandoned her. Then she met that war hero. What a waste that had been; years in Cornwall like a prison sentence, all those teaching applications rejected. Quite how this one had come through, she didn't know, just been glad to get out of that living hell.

She looked at Jonathan, wondering if it were wrong to seek fulfilment in his achievements; if he becomes a success, would that be enough?

SEVEN

Elysian Fields

THE NEXT DAY JONATHAN RETURNED TO OXFORD on the train and carried his few belongings up to his Rooms. He looked at his stuff with a new eye; the only thing he could be proud of was his special tool case. But even that caused him a moment of despair, for it held the tools of his trade, the picklocks and the stethoscope that he had used to open the safe at Mountbeck. He had thought that the task was all above board, but look what trouble it had got him into. He took the tool case into the bedroom and slipped it under the bed. He recalled the embarrassing encounter with Hilary, shaking his head in disbelief.

Returning to the sitting room, he was newly astonished at his good fortune. After he had put his stuff away, he sat down and wondered just how secure he might be. Surely the de Quincys wouldn't try anything else; he had no interest in using his knowledge against them. He had learned a valuable lesson; powerful people would use you for their own ends and you would be treated well only as long as they needed you.

On the other hand Count Paolo Passaglietti had treated him kindly, even driving him in his car away from Mountbeck to Thirsk station. The Count had given him his Bank's business card with the address in San Marino, telling him to get in touch if he ever needed a friend. When Jonathan saw the address he remembered the Bearer Bond. He had taken it from Arthur's safe to convince Sailor to spill the beans on the Gang's meeting. He hadn't meant to keep it but everything had happened so fast that he was back at Mountbeck before he realized that he still had it. He had shown it to the Count who had offered to cash it for him. So he had a cheque for a thousand pounds in his pocket. He began to feel a bit more secure.

He noticed a new folder lying on the desk. He opened it and saw a set of visiting cards and a detailed list of instructions. There was something authoritarian about the instructions; he smiled; it must be Jason at work. He sat down and read the document, finding a lot of helpful information. There was even an ABC of Oxford with a key showing the main points of interest.

He saw that a bank was not too far away. He decided to get some fresh air and set off to cash the Count's cheque. When he got there, it turned out to be the local branch of a national Bank. It seemed designed to intimidate its customers, the tall woodwork and wrought iron grilles allowing only a small glimpse of the staff. He stood at one of the narrow openings. A young woman arrived giving him the impression that whatever she had been doing was far more important than attending to his needs. When he presented the cheque she appeared to be stunned.

"I think you'd better see the Manager," she said eventually in a nasal voice.

Jonathan was shown into a small and rather cramped office. A middle-aged man was studying the cheque, giving Jonathan the impression that he had never seen one before. He looked up and cleared his throat.

"This cheque is drawn on Croftts Bank. I can't honour it immediately, I'm afraid; there will be a long clearance period."

Jonathan said that he didn't understand. "Is there something wrong with it?"

"Oh no, sir, quite the opposite," the manager smirked. "Croftts is a private Bank in London, serving a very special clientele."

Jonathan realised with a start that he was a more important person than a young man coming off the street. He recalled seeing the documents that Sir Roger had brought to Mountbeck. They had been fakes of course, but they would have to be superficially genuine. Some of them had been from the same Bank.

The manager was scratching his head. "Actually, sir, there is a satellite of Croffts Bank here in Oxford, to assist some of the, well, wealthier undergraduates. Perhaps you should try there. Just a minute, sir," he muttered, taking a folder from his desk. "Yes, here it is." He took a sheet of the Bank's paper and carefully wrote out the address, folded the paper and proffered it to Jonathan as if it was a valuable gift.

When Jonathan got to the address, he thought at first that it was some kind of joke, for the door was firmly closed. He looked around and eventually spotted a small white button. He pressed it and a female voice said, "Yes?" with that assumption of superiority that always irritated him.

Jonathan was at a loss; he thought this was the strangest Bank he had ever heard of.

"I have a cheque that I would like to cash."

"Which Bank is it drawn upon?"

"Croffts Bank Limited," Jonathan read out.

There was a buzz and the door opened. He went in and found what looked like a Day Room in a country house. It reminded him of Victoria's home at Frodsham. There were flower arrangements and pictures in elegant frames on the walls. They were not reproduction Constables, he was sure of that.

A door opened and a man entered. He was dressed in a black jacket and striped trousers, with a gold watch chain stretched across his waistcoat. Jonathan wished he had worn his Chaseman suit.

The man waved Jonathan to a chair at an antique desk and sat down on the other side.

"Now, sir," said the banker, "how may I be of assistance?"

Jonathan took out the cheque and handed it to the man, who extracted a small pair of glasses from his waistcoat pocket and attached them to his nose. Jonathan had never seen this particular practice before; the spring-loaded mechanism fascinated him.

The man looked up.

"May I ask whether you are personally acquainted with Count Passaglietti?"

Jonathan thought about the question, perhaps for too long.

"I've met him several times, but really only on business."

"I see, sir, and what business would that be? You see, a personal cheque for such a large amount[24] is really quite unusual and the Count has not, ah, given us instructions."

Jonathan was getting nervous for he could hardly explain the circumstances to a stranger.

"I'm sure the Count would vouch for me if you ask him," he said.

"I see, sir; you would not object if we were to make such enquiries?"

Jonathan shrugged. "No, I don't need the money right now, I just want it to earn some interest."

"What I propose, sir, is that we open an account here on a temporary basis until we have spoken to the Count."

He opened a drawer and pulled out a form, saying, "I will need some personal details, of course."

Jonathan remembered the new cards Jason had left for him and put one on the table. The words 'Galdraith Scholar' stood out from the rest of the text.

The man picked up the card and smiled. "Oh, this is quite a different set of affairs, sir; now I know who you are, I can dispense with most of the other formalities."

Jonathan left the bank the proud owner of a cheque book, a savings account with a thousand pound balance and a small card with some telephone numbers on it. He was to contact any of the numbers should he be 'in need of our services at any time'.

Jonathan walked back to his rooms thinking about the huge difference between the two banking experiences. He could get used to having an account at a bank like Croftts, he thought with a grin. And he realised

---

24 A thousand pounds represented about a quarter of the value of a nice detached house.

that his position as the Galdraith Scholar gave him advantages far beyond having a nice set of Rooms at Oxford University. By the time he got back to his Rooms the threats posed by the enemies he had made in London had faded into the background.

Arthur Salmon in his new identity as Percy Thomas sat disconsolately in his office. The door carried the words 'Executive Manager' but Arthur thought he was more like a baby-sitter, since all the floor action was over-seen by a professional group who more or less ignored him. Certainly he had to ensure that all the day to day aspects of a business in London were observed, but that wasn't much, just the occasional paperwork. He was only involved with the gambling side of things when the day's takings were installed in the safe. He had acquired an old Champion safe from a contact in the Isle of Dogs, got a good price and soaked the club for the cost of a new one. No one would know; Yanks were out of their depth in London, weren't they? He had grown a small moustache, trimmed just so, and had dyed his hair a rather flashy black. He thought with a lopsided grin that he looked a bit like that film star, Ronald Colman.

Jonathan's eye fell on the blue envelope on the mantelpiece. He picked it up and re-read Victoria's letter. 'Well,' he thought, 'I have a telephone and I can try it out,' so he dialled the operator. When she answered, he asked for the Frodsham number.

He recognised the voice that answered; it was Thomas, the de Quincys' man.

"Thomas, this is Jonathan Hare."

"Yes, sir, we were expecting you to ring. A moment, please sir, I believe your party may be available."

Jonathan recalled that there was more to Thomas than met the eye. After a few moments, he heard footsteps and then Victoria's voice.

"Jonathan, Jonathan Hare?" she whispered.

He was reminded of the time in the Savoy when she had called out to him using the same words.

He waited, feeling apprehensive about talking to a de Quincy.

"Say something, Jonathan, please," she almost begged.

He relented.

"I got your note, Victoria; what can I do for you?"

The strangely remote tone in his voice took her aback. There was a pause, during which he thought he could hear sobbing.

"Would you come and see me, Jonathan, please?" she said eventually. Her voice was muffled.

He thought she must have suffered terribly from the break-up of the engagement, for there was none of that haughtiness with which she had once spoken to him.

"Only, it can't be here, you understand?"

He decoded that message.

"Can you come to the White Horse? I'll be riding there this evening when it's cooler. It's so beautiful up there, you can see for miles."

He remembered how much she loved that place, so strangely atmospheric, the ancient Ridgeway stretching away, tracing the route taken by shepherds and travellers for thousands of years.

"Do come, Jonathan, I can send the car."

This was a considerate gesture, for the hill up to the Ridgeway was steep, certainly too much for a bike, he thought with a grin.

"Could the car meet me at Abingdon College in Oxford?"

There were muffled voices; Victoria confirmed and they agreed a time.

Arthur Salmon never knew when Joe would appear; the man from Las Vegas spent his time travelling around the world and felt comfortable dropping in whenever he was passing through London. Joe was always complimentary, the words dropping off his lips with ease, although once or twice Arthur wondered whether Joe was actually conscious of the phrases he was using. Arthur was always 'looking great today', the Club was 'doing great thanks to you, Arthur', and so on.

But Joe was on top of everything. He had heard that someone had found out about the bearer bonds from San Marino and the threat to their operation that this implied. Sterling Control Regulations remained in force and they couldn't afford to risk their financing structure. So Joe had looked pointedly at Arthur. "It's your problem, fix it," was all he'd said.

Today, however, Arthur had some other business to discuss.

"Joe, the other night we took a marker off a toff, a bit more than usual; the idiot was drunk as a skunk," he said, employing an Americanism he had picked up from the floor staff.

"Thing is, we need to be careful; the toff is, well, a bit rich for our blood; he could cause us trouble. I've received some hints to let him off, but you told me never to do that without your say-so."

Joe turned his eyes on Arthur; they were suddenly a different colour. "How much?"

Arthur told him, converting it into US dollars.

"No," was all Joe said.

Arthur hadn't previously had to argue with Joe, so he persisted.

"Joe, it's heavy money over here. Thing is, people who are as well connected as the toff, they've got clout, friends in high places, they can pull strings."

Joe's eyes made Arthur think of a snake sizing up its prey.

"Keep it; it'll come in useful."

The matter was closed; Joe had made it painfully clear who was the boss.

The incident reminded Arthur that he had far too little to do in the club. He increasingly found himself recalling that Jonathan Hare was the real cause of his dilemma. His attempt to deal with him once and for all by dragging the little runt to Dockland had gone badly wrong; the whole thing had been a police trap from the beginning. And as if that wasn't enough, the press had carried a report of the new Galdraith Scholar, none other than Mister Jonathan Hare. Arthur spat into his wastepaper basket. The days of enforced idleness had caused his resentment to grow;

eventually he put out a few feelers through one of his private companies and had a tail put on Jonathan.

"I'll get him one of these days," he said out loud. He felt better already.

Jonathan's telephone rang; it was Jason.

"Mr. Hare, sir, there is a large motor car here for you."

On an impulse, he put on the hat that old Bronsky had given him and went down the stairs and across the quadrangle to the Porter's Lodge. Sure enough, the de Quincy Rolls Royce was waiting. He walked carefully to the car. When he saw the driver, he stopped in alarm; it was the blue suited man who served Sir Roger so assiduously.

"Don't worry, Mr. Hare, you're safe with me; Miss Victoria has sworn me to secrecy. Sir Roger has assigned me to look after her, and she says this is just part of it!"

He smiled at Jonathan, who sighed, recalling one of his mother's sayings, 'in for a penny, in for a pound'.

As the great car drifted silently away, he realised that he had never asked the man's name. He discovered that it was 'Martin, just Martin, sir', reminding him of that day at Frodsham when he hadn't known how to address Thomas.

Hilary Magnette had come out of the College Library and spotted Jonathan as he headed for the Lodge. He was wearing that hat again, the one that made him look a little too much like a young Dick Powell. She walked quickly after him, hoping to clear up any misunderstanding and was just in time to see him get in the Rolls Royce and drive away. She stopped, not knowing what to think. Wasn't that family crest on the car door the same as the one on the envelope? Once more she felt ashamed for throwing herself at someone of his class. Whatever had she been thinking? She sighed, getting annoyed, either at him or herself, she wasn't quite sure.

The Rolls Royce eased its way through the golden beauty of the country-side, its hedgerows heavy with summer growth. They passed driveways with country houses half hidden by arching avenues of trees. Suddenly they were at the crossroad at the foot of the scarp leading to the White Horse, the arm of the signpost pointed sharply upwards. With exquisite humour, it carried the words 'The Downs'.

The road was little more than a track, and the car took its time climb-ing to the summit. When they got there, a girl was dismounting. It was Victoria. She waved to Martin and he got out and held the horse.

Jonathan pulled down the brim of his hat as Victoria approached the car; he thought she looked a little better than when he last saw her in London; the ride had put some colour into her face, and when she took off the helmet, her hair was loose. But she was still thin and there were dark circles under her eyes. As she got in, he slid into the far corner of the car, looking at her from beneath the brim of the hat.

For a moment she was taken aback, then she started to laugh. "Oh Jonathan, what am I to do with you, I'd know you anywhere, you can't fool me!"

She reached out and took his hand. "That's the first time I've laughed since..." she stopped.

He squeezed her hand in encouragement.

"Since I broke off the engagement," she finished in a rush.

Her eyes were wide. "See, you've done me good already; I haven't been able to say that before."

He hoped the rest of the conversation would be this easy.

She was fidgeting, but he couldn't help her; she had something to say and he would have to wait.

"Please just listen. You don't have to say anything, just be my friend."

She stopped and bit her lip for a while.

She took a breath. "I never wanted to marry Robert, you know, but there was so much pressure and all the other girls were announcing, and

Mother was so persuasive, and I thought Robert would be a gentleman and not force me against my will."

She was blushing. Jonathan squeezed her hand again; he was surprised that he felt a surge of affection for her; he had never seen her so vulnerable.

"But I couldn't marry him after I found out what he was really like, could I?"

Jonathan was lost; he shrugged.

"Oh, of course, you wouldn't know," she said, looking into the distance. "He made one of the house servants pregnant and didn't take care to look after her, poor girl; she's disappeared and now no one can find her. She went away to live with a relative somewhere."

He took off his hat and moved closer to her. "What did your mother say about it?"

"Oh, Jonathan, you know her, once on the stage, always a performer. She thinks it's what happens in those families; 'par for the course' I think she said."

There was a pause. He sensed that there was more to come. It dawned on him that she needed comfort, so he put his arm lightly around her shoulders. She glanced quickly at him and settled against him.

"Do you remember when we talked in the garden at my father's place in London?" she muttered.

He squeezed her shoulder in confirmation.

He remembered being annoyed with her, thinking that she had betrayed him with that act at the table that gave away his real identity. Their conversation had been difficult. She had eventually reacted explosively, saying something about 'hating her life because it was all so arranged'.

He thought he'd better not open that door. To avoid the issue he said, "I remember you calling me an idiot!"

She pulled away and stared at him. "Yes, well, I was angry. I thought you would be more sympathetic."

She settled back against him. "Sometimes, when one is angry, one tells the truth. I hated the Season; my mother was so excited, it was like being back on centre stage for her, all those dances and house parties, dresses and photographs. Did you see us in the *Tatler*?"

He looked at her in amazement.

"Didn't your father tell you *anything* about what I was doing for him?"

She shook her head.

"Well, I certainly didn't have time to read the *Tatler*!"

She pouted, and he realised that she was still wrapped up in her own concerns. He was getting a dose of his own medicine for once; he would have to wait for her to continue.

"I didn't realise that all my so-called friends would take against me when I broke off the engagement. Apparently it's the worst crime a girl can commit. They say I'll be shunned from now on; no man will risk asking me to marry him; it's just too embarrassing. What am I to do, Jonathan?" she asked.

She had pulled away from him again and he could see the plea in her eyes.

He was appalled, not knowing how to answer; he would have to play for time.

"What does your father say?" he tried.

She slumped back in the seat in despair. "Oh, him, he just tells me that my mother must be the one to tell me what to do. Can't blame him really, it'd be different if he was my real father," she said unemotionally.

It came as a shock to Jonathan but it explained a lot of strange things about the de Quincys that he had noted but not understood at the time. He had almost never seen Sir Roger and Lady Antonia together, and she had never mentioned Sir Roger in any of their icy conversations.

"I don't understand," he said.

She leant forward and looked at him closely. "I was a few months old when my mother married father. My mother simply won't discuss it; she tells me that it was all for the best and that my life is so much nicer than it would have been. At least I have a father, not like so many children during the war who never knew their fathers, just a telegram and a newspaper cutting if they were lucky."

Jonathan had gone cold, remembering the mystery of his own father; his mother would also never speak about it, and there was that strange entry in somebody's file: 'Father killed in the war'.

A silence fell while they were both lost in their own thoughts. It didn't seem strange to either of them that they were comforting each other.

Jonathan emerged from his reverie and said, "You need a job, something to take your mind off your problems. Didn't your father want you to work at the Society?"

She looked at him in surprise. "Whatever gave you that idea?"

He shrugged. "He left me with that impression, but it's sometimes hard to know, when he's playing his games."

She had her arm round his waist and her head on his shoulder.

"Playing games, whatever do you mean?" she murmured.

He remembered that Sir Roger hadn't disclosed his real job to her.

He trod water. "He likes to come at a problem indirectly, don't you think?"

She nodded, and he relaxed again.

"This is nice; I like it when you have your arms around me," she said, although he could hardly hear her. She pulled his head down and kissed him lightly. He was relieved that there wasn't the raw animal feeling that had come when Charmaine had kissed him. Victoria's kiss was one of friendship; her lips were dry and only slightly puckered. As he looked at her she opened her eyes, and they both laughed with their mouths pressed together.

"I've always liked you, Jonathan. Will you be my friend, come and see me sometimes?"

He explained about Oxford. "But once I'm settled there, we can have afternoon tea, perhaps?" She knew he was teasing, and laughed.

Then she turned serious. "I don't know where you live; somewhere in the town, of course. How will I get in touch?"

He felt the ground moving under his feet, and said hurriedly, "I have my own rooms in Oxford. I'll telephone you and let you know when I get settled. It's better that we meet away from probing eyes!"

She put her hand to her mouth and grinned. "You make it sound exciting!"

As the Rolls Royce conveyed Jonathan back to Abingdon College he thought about Victoria. He had felt comfortable with her; there wasn't the same tension that was just under the surface when he was with Hilary. And he had no reason to blame Victoria for what her father had done; she was in the dark about what really went on at the Society. He thought back to the first time he was asked to go there, with that test of his technical abilities in the room with the observation window. Sir Roger had presented it as security to protect the Society's treasures, but Jonathan now realised it was really an interrogation room. Sir Roger used the Society as a front to conceal its real purpose and his family would think of it as just a harmless and rather boring scientific museum.

Hilary Magnette had not been as forthcoming with her father as she usually was. He knew her well enough to sense that something had happened to cause her introspection, so unlike her. He had an idea that it had something to do with the Hare fellow who might not have been happy with Hilary's choice of decor. He had given her free rein, no expense spared; he had to do justice to the College; those pompous Masters were just waiting to find something to criticize. He had resisted their attempts to make Abingdon a clone of all the other architectural wonders. His argument that modern technology needed an appropriate context had apparently won the day; although he had a suspicion that influence to quell their hostility had been applied from above.

Hilary was still angry with herself. She had assumed that she could toy with the new Scholar; after all, he would be in her father's debt, and that would create some interesting opportunities.

She was proud of her father for achieving so much, with a Life Peerage to crown it all. When her mother had died last year, she had been so sad for him, glad that her mother's suffering was over, but conscious of the terrible gap left in their lives. She had grown much closer to her father during this last year; he had retired when his industrial empire had been nationalized and his interests were now focused on the College. He had more time for her and had actually come to a ballet lesson or two. He hadn't been very nice about some of the boys, with no understanding that not all young men were rugby-playing monsters.

She was startled when he broke the silence. "Did Hare like the rooms?"

She was glad of a chance to vent her annoyance. "Just another over-compensating male, Dad; made me take out the curtains and hated the pillows. Poor old Jason will have to change that headboard again!"

Jonathan had gone up several notches in her father's estimation, not that he would ever reveal that to Hilary.

She just had to broach the subject otherwise it would drive her crazy. "This young man, Dad, what do you know about him?"

Her father had had some occasional thoughts along the same lines.

"Why do you ask, dear?"

She wondered what to say, but ploughed ahead. "I thought he was, well, just an ordinary fellow, you know, but he must have some connections, come from a good family, or something like that. You know Jason, nothing is going to fool him, but he..."

She stopped, trying to think how to express herself. Her father was watching with secret amusement.

"As soon as I introduced them, Dad, Jason sort of came to attention, very strange, and from then always called him 'sir', as if he was on the parade ground. And," she seemed to realise this in mid sentence,

"Jonathan spoke to him as though that was how he expected to be treated!" She was proud of that observation.

Her father noticed that she had used his first name.

Jonathan was reading the instructions for the Galdraith Scholar with increasing anticipation. Someone had spent hours setting out detailed instructions and guidelines for just about every aspect of his life.

"They'll tell me how to wipe my backside next," he thought with a grin.

He was glad of the monthly schedules, although there seemed to be far more social occasions than academic. There was a page written in a different style that particularly fascinated him. Apparently he had an account at a tailor's in somewhere called 'The Turl'.

He got out the ABC of Oxford that showed all the colleges, hotels and places of interest. He found 'Turl Street' in the index; it was a small stub road running between Broad Street and the High. He knew Oxford well, and had often biked there, but there had been no reason to go into those expensive areas before. There were plenty of places for the ordinary shopper; Burtons and Marks and Spencer's in the Cornmarket for instance.

He would require a dinner jacket; he smiled when he recalled Germaine calling it a 'smoking' when he wore that one at Mountbeck. He looked at his bed and the new belongings laid out there. A cheque book and several cards that gave him access to people who were once beyond his imagination. And now he would have a wardrobe of clothes too. He decided to telephone the tailor's shop in 'The Turl' and discovered another pleasant surprise.

"Oh yes, Mr. Hare, sir, we were hoping you would ring. We have a list of the Scholar's requirements, sir, and when may we expect you?"

Jonathan had some difficulty keeping his amusement out of his voice. This new world he had entered certainly provided some comic relief. What a difference status and money made; the card he had presented at Croftts Bank had just been a piece of paper, but it had caused an amazing change in the way that he had been received. And as the Scholar he was now a person of sufficient importance to warrant a politeness that he certainly wouldn't have received if he had dared to go in off the street. He said he'd be there in half an hour and put on the charcoal grey suit that had opened so many doors during his time in London. He put his cheque book in his pocket. It made him feel good.

When he got there, he noticed that the shop sign above the windows contained the word 'bespoke'. He wondered how many years that word had been used to indicate quality and expense. A middle-aged man came forward, sporting a tape measure around his neck. They consulted the list and began a process of selection of material and measurement that Jonathan found quite personal. He supposed that one got used to strange men's hands running over one's body, but it was a new experience for him. Certain measurements and questions caused him acute embarrassment, but he realised that perfection in dress required attention to such detail.

The tailor steadily ticked off the items, all the while eyeing Jonathan's suit.

"That's a beautiful suit sir; a Chaseman's if I'm not mistaken. Have you had it a while, sir?"

Jonathan decided a neutral sound was his best answer; he had no idea what the tailor's remark meant.

"Now, sir, for the dinner jacket; we have several styles," he said, opening a large book.

Jonathan spotted one that was similar to the one that Travis had found for him at Mountbeck. He said it would do and could he have it as soon as possible. The tailor made a note.

"Well sir, thank you; that seems to be all we need today. Come back in a week, sir, and we'll be able to do the fittings."

Jonathan realised that making a suit to fit must be as complicated as building a model or designing test equipment. He took out the chequebook, but the man simply smiled, "Oh no, sir, everything will be entered into the account. For the Scholar, sir," he added, seeing Jonathan's confusion.

By the time Victoria arrived home, she felt hurt and angry. When her mother confronted her, she said, "I'm tired, Mother, why don't we continue the inquisition tomorrow."

It was as rude as she had ever been, and it took Lady Antonia by surprise. Before she could respond, Victoria had left the Day Room and disappeared up the stairs. In her room, she took off her riding clothes and looked at herself in the mirror. She was thinner than before, but still well proportioned and womanly. She knew how attractive she had looked in London when she was dressed in her finery. Then she recalled that Jonathan had seen her that night at the Savoy and had been so stern with her, not at all impressed with her as a woman. And tonight was so strange, he had done everything she asked, been gentle and kind, and had put his arms around her, but, well, he hadn't shown that he wanted anything more than that.

"What is wrong with me?" she wondered.

She replayed the whole day, his remoteness on the telephone, and how hard she had to work to get him to see her.

"Even had to send the car for him," she snorted.

She wondered why he had to make fun of her, reminding her of that night in the Savoy, stupid hat, stupid 'private eye'.

The sudden remembrance of that occasion came as a shock; he had been so forceful with her and she had felt something new; he had never spoken to her that way before and it had been really quite exciting. She put on her night things and got into bed.

As she dozed, she tried to recreate the feeling of his arms around her. She came fully awake with the realisation that, behind his kindness there was something else, a reserve, no, more than that. She sat up, trying to recall his side of the conversation. She had been so happy to talk to him about her own problems that she had hardly listened to him. What had he said about her father? Something about whether her father had told her about the job that Jonathan was doing for him? There had been anger there, she thought. And hadn't Jonathan said something about her father 'playing games'? Again she sensed that Jonathan had been angry, but not with her, with her father.

She lay back with a smile on her face. No wonder he had been so distant in the car, but it wasn't her, after all. That night she had her first good night's sleep since the disaster with Robert.

She dreamed a strangely modern version of Tennyson's story of 'Gareth and Lynette', where Gareth is so badly treated by the Lady Lynette, and how that Lady fails to recognise his knightly virtues, to her own cost, perhaps.

EIGHT

The Ties that Bind

During World War II British propaganda exhorted people to 'Make Do and Mend'. Over the years the British developed a mindset similar to 'string syndrome', a term coined to describe the behaviour of concentration camp victims who picked up and saved every tiny scrap of material. While conditions in wartime Britain never reached the horrendous depredation of the camps, patriotic citizens actually hoarded string in kitchen table drawers and ironed wrapping paper so that it could be used again. Envelopes were reused many times over and letters written not only on both sides of the paper but at right angles across the script. In these conditions, which prevailed for far longer than the hostilities, people began to develop an unhealthy attachment to what little they had. For decades after the War, British people could never throw anything away. As to financial capital, it was more than a psychological prop; it became something to be held on to at all costs. Money took on an intrinsic value; people often knew to the last penny how much they had in their pocket.

During his outing with Victoria Jonathan had forgotten about the threats that were just over the horizon. But back in his Rooms, he began to feel the weight of them again. It was time to take stock, he thought. So he sat on his bed and came up with a balance sheet in his head.

He was the Galdraith Scholar and this meant that he could count on support from that quarter. He had one nice suit and an understanding of how it could open doors for him. And now he had an account with a huge amount of money in it, and in a high class Bank at that. He couldn't comprehend what such a large amount actually meant. It was clear though that it would sustain him in just about any set of circumstances; he would have to guard it with his life. He grimaced at that thought.

On the negative side, he couldn't be sure that the threat from the de Quincys was out of play. And there was still the possibility that Arthur was free and able to have another go at him. What he needed was some form of physical protection, which was all very well, but where could he get that?

Eventually his thoughts turned to Jason in the Porter's Lodge. Jason had made it clear that he was charged with personal responsibility for the Galdraith Scholar. Perhaps he would know what to do.

Officer Cadets at Sandhurst[25] who suffered under Sergeant Major Jason credited him with an eye for detail that bordered on the miraculous. So it was not surprising when his sense of order was disturbed by the too frequent appearance of a man in the Isis Book Shop just opposite the College. The man had been occupying a chair near a window and since this had begun before the official start of the Michaelmas Term and with Mr. Hare being the only student in residence Jason had decided that it must be him who was the target. He picked up the telephone and rang the Scholar's number.

"Mr. Hare, sir," he said, "would you be free to come down to the Lodge for a moment?"

Jason's call coming at that particular moment was a shock. And Jason's request wasn't phrased as an option either. He hurried down and slipped through the half door into the Lodge.

Jason took him to a side window that looked over the street.

---

25   The Royal Military Academy Sandhurst has produced officers for the British Army since 1741. Those selected to the military instructional staff are held in the highest esteem.

"I believe, sir, that someone has set up an observation post across the way in the Book Shop."

Jonathan saw a man wearing a blue jacket apparently reading a book. The light was reflecting off the covering on the man's shoulders. Jonathan had a shock; it was a 'donkey jacket', the all too familiar garb in Dockland. He recalled once asking Harry about it. Harry had replied with a conspiratorial grin, "It's what they all wear around here; keeps you warm and has a poacher's pocket, just the ticket for getting loose cargo out of the docks."

So, Jonathan thought, someone from Dockland has put a watcher on me. But who? The only person who came to mind was Arthur Salmon. So perhaps Arthur *had* escaped the raid on the warehouse. He forced himself to think back to that day when he opened the safe for Bert. He hadn't known then that it was Arthur's hiding place for all those bearer bonds he had stolen from the Gang. He'd had plenty of time to work that out while locked in the store room with Jane and had used it to convince Sailor to cooperate. Arthur would know that by now; which would be why Arthur wanted to get his hands on him. A cold sweat started. Jonathan told himself not to panic, but that was easier said than done. First the de Quincy brothers had tried to harm him and now Arthur was after him. He had to sit down, feeling nauseated.

"Are you all right, sir?" Jason asked.

Jonathan could only nod; he got up and walked unsteadily back to the safety of his Rooms.

Jason considered the situation. He was responsible to Lord Galdraith for Jonathan's wellbeing and it was now clear that there was some sort of danger. Jason scratched his head; this wasn't the Army and the arrangements he could have made in a military environment didn't apply here. He would have to get some advice, and quickly.

Jonathan sank morosely into his chair, the one that only a few days ago he had been so happy to have. The image of that donkey jacket wouldn't go away; the man may only be watching, but it proved that Arthur must have found out where he was. Of course, that wouldn't have been difficult; there had been an article on the back pages of the national press about the award of the Scholarship.

He was in some sort of danger, but it wasn't immediate, just a threat. Jason had already shown that he was watching out for him. He felt a little better. He recalled Harry's amusement about the donkey jacket. But that was it! Harry would be the best person to ask for help; he knew the ropes in Dockland and probably could work out some sort of counter to Arthur's plan. He picked up the telephone and asked for Harry's number.

Lady Hecate was thinking about her son and how she had dismissed him. She had retired to her favourite place, rarely seen by even the most exalted visitors. She called it the Lavender Room; she had chosen that shade of light purple for the décor over the objections, muted though they were, of her decorators. She moved around the room with an elegance that came naturally to her, absently examining the ornaments and pictures that usually gave her so much pleasure. She had only to telephone the right person to set in motion inquiries regarding the Club that her son had so stupidly patronized. She was intent on selecting just the right person. Roger de Quincy wasn't an option, but she knew others in similar clandestine positions that were indebted to her. She decided and, as was her habit, telephoned immediately.

Lady Hecate's contact occupied an anonymous office in the top floor of a glowering building on Northumberland Avenue. If the good citizens of England knew what his job was, they might have written scathing letters to the *Times*, forgetting that even in the best democracies there are dark deeds to be done. He was instantly alert, for he had already been briefed on the national interest in that particular club and the danger it represented. He was in a quandary, for this information was not to be shared and yet he was more than obliged to satisfy Lady Hecate. He decided to buy some time; he would push some buttons in a social setting. He arranged to meet with Superintendent Alistair Henderson – "Have some lunch, pick your brains?" He knew the superintendent would be flattered. What he didn't know was that Alistair had already been assigned a watching brief by the Commissioner personally, nor that the Commissioner had said, "No action yet. Wait until we can get the whole set-up, roots and all."

Harry Sparrow was pleased to hear from Jonathan and yet alarmed at his tone of voice. Harry knew him well enough by now to sense that something was wrong; the lad almost never showed his real feelings. Harry had been annoyed at first, thinking that Jonathan was a stuck-up brat, what with his posh accent and good manners. But Harry had learned that there was a lot more to him than that. The fact that Arthur Salmon's name hadn't been among those captured in the raid probably meant that the rozzers had him stowed away somewhere. So when Jonathan told him about the watcher in Oxford, Harry was at first lost for words. He could see why Jonathan would assume that it must be Arthur's doing, but he could come up with nothing helpful.

"Leave it with me, mate," said Harry.

Jonathan noticed that Harry had used the familiar term 'mate' for the first time; from Harry this was a compliment, well, more than that. It signalled that Harry would put his considerable East End resources onto the problem. For a minute or two Jonathan felt better but the threat was still there. He poured himself some more tea.

People in Lady Hecate's position are seldom motivated by the desire for 'filthy lucre' since they will have been born and raised in an environment where money is never an issue. Many families had acquired wealth over the hundreds of years during which the Empire had expanded and had been advised by the very best financial establishments in the City[26]. Their assets had grown, sometimes exponentially. For those families money

---

26   The City of London occupies just one square mile of Greater London, but
has for centuries been the financial centre of the world, wielding huge power
mostly behind the scenes.

had long ago ceased to have any intrinsic value; it was merely a lubricant to further their interests.

William Magnette, now Lord Galdraith thanks to his success in industry, had only recently accumulated his assets. To Lady Hecate's circle, he was looked upon as being 'nouveau riche' and certainly not 'People Like Us'[27]. So it was more than a surprise to Lady Hecate's friends when he was welcomed into her circle. In fact, and for no reason that they could discern, he appeared to be especially favoured; comments had been made, but never in Lady Hecate's hearing. Had her friends been more alert they might have realised that his stature in her eyes came from his ability to explain little publicised happenings in industry and commerce that she would either support or have contained to further her own interests.

Lady Hecate's contact in Northumberland Avenue liked to use the nom de guerre 'Sir James' and to hold some of his meetings at a restaurant in the City where he was known by that name. Superintendent Alistair Henderson arrived there as instructed and Carlos, the head waiter, escorted him to the table.

"Here is your guest, Sir James, just as you described him."

Sir James waved Alistair to the chair opposite. Alistair had to struggle to keep his face straight. 'Sir James' was dressed in a black jacket, a high wing collar, and black waistcoat complete with gold watch chain. It was perfect camouflage. Looking around, nearly every other diner was wearing the same uniform. Alistair thought it was a good job he'd been told to wear plain clothes; if he had worn his dark blue serge with the silver crown he would have stood out like a sore thumb and probably scared off half the clientele. Lunch was over before Sir James opened the subject. He seemed to be more interested in the pattern in the tablecloth.

---

27   This term, abbreviated to 'PLU', is relatively new. People of Lady Hecate's ilk would never allow it to pass their lips; whether a person was of the proper class and breeding would be obvious to them.

"I picked up a rumour the other day, Alistair; friend of mine visited a new club, just opened apparently, near South Audley Street. He thought it a bit rum, don't you know, what did he say, staff too professional, décor too nouveau, reminded him of Las Vegas, somehow."

Alistair hoped he had got control of himself in time. He would have to tread water.

Sir James went on, "Made him feel uneasy, not a gentleman's place like; well, Alistair, you know where our sort of chap goes, what?"

There was a pause. Alistair waited for the knife to be inserted.

"Pity if the wrong sort of people got a toe-hold, Alistair." This time Sir James was looking directly at him.

"Indeed, Sir James," he said, "would you like us to keep an eye on it?"

Sir James smiled. "Might be as well to know who runs the place, uncover the wraps a bit, what?"

"I'll see what I can do, Sir James, behind the scenes of course."

But he had understood the implication; enquiries in that field might yield results. Sir James had also signalled by his interest that someone in the highest circles had expressed concern. It didn't take a giant intellectual leap to guess that some highly placed idiot had signed a note beyond his means.

Harry Sparrow's contacts in the Dockland underworld would have impressed even 'Sir James', although he would have thought their pedigree left much to be desired. Harry's business with the Grey Gang had always been at arm's-length; he disapproved of their methods and disliked Arthur Salmon more than any of them. When his friend Bert Coleman had vanished into thin air, Harry was sure it was Arthur's doing.

He thought back to the night when Jonathan had opened Arthur's safe. Bert had been beside himself with worry; what had he said, then? Something like: "Arthur would sack me for sure." So perhaps Arthur had something in the safe more important than mere money, something that he couldn't afford anyone to know about.

Harry recalled that he and Bert had been in another room having a cuppa to pass the time when Jonathan announced that he'd got the safe open. It would have been possible for the lad to have seen inside the safe. And if Arthur suspected Jonathan had done that, the lad was a target for sure. It would explain a lot about the kidnapping.

First things first, Harry told himself; he had to find Arthur. A Cockney like Harry knew where to go for information; down the pub, sit at the bar, talk to the barmaid, have a giggle, and who knew what else. It took him a while and it wasn't until he dropped into the 'Leg o' Mutton' right next to Smithfield Market that he got a break. Rosie was her usual self, Cupid's bow lipstick and a pouter pigeon chest that brought tears to some men's eyes. She winked at Harry over the inevitable cigarette dangling from the corner of her mouth. He waited until the bar traffic died down a bit. Rosie was well in with the Grey Gang; Harry couldn't remember which one of the bosses she had been shacked up with before the raid. He teased her about it.

"Must be lonely these nights, Rosie," he said, raising an eyebrow.

"You askin'?" she said with a lopsided grin.

Harry and Rosie had known each other far too long, so the moment was allowed to pass.

Rosie leant over the bar and muttered in her tobacco baritone, "You want to talk to Flora about lonely, damn woman's driving me out of my mind."

Harry told himself to keep calm.

"Really, why's that?" he asked, offhandedly.

"Didn't you hear? That rat Arthur escaped the round-up and now he's nowhere to be found." Rosie left to serve a customer, while Harry tried not to look too interested. But he needn't have worried, Rosie came right back.

"But he's not that far away, I reckon, holed up somewhere; one of his outfits found an old safe for him, bloody heavy according to Bill Enright. They had a terrible time getting it up to some place in the West

End. Bill was still sweating like a pig when he came in here; downed three pints in a hurry, I can tell you."

Harry had a hard time controlling himself; he knew he had to sit still for a while and pass some time with Rosie, otherwise she might realise just what she had said and who she had said it to.

Rosie, for her part, had seized the opportunity to drop the hint to Harry. She'd tried to put up with Flora's endless whining, but enough was enough! As far as she was concerned, Arthur and Flora deserved each other and the sooner they got back together the sooner she'd be able to get on with her own life. And not with Harry either, she thought with a grin.

Towards the end of the nineteenth century, Queen Victoria bestowed a Dukedom upon the Grosvenor family, already wealthy and landed, with thousands of acres of countryside in England and Scotland. The family is an old one, but made a giant leap forward in 1677, when Sir Thomas Grosvenor married Mary Davies, an heiress of 500 acres of rural land on the outskirts of London. As London grew, this property became the source of the family's immense wealth for it developed into the fashionable areas of Mayfair and Belgravia. Hundreds of roads, squares and buildings bear their family names and titles including Grosvenor Square, Belgrave Square, North Audley Street, South Audley Street, and Davies Street. Part of the family's success is attributable to the fact that the best of its Mayfair and Belgravia properties have remained in the family, being leased to wealthy residents. Eaton Square, where Lady Hecate resided, might be the jewel in the crown of Belgravia.

As in all well managed leasehold operations, a change of occupant requires the approval of the property owner. But the Westminster holdings are so numerous that, from time to time, such changes take place in a deliberately clandestine manner and are not immediately detected by the management.

Back in his house, Harry thought about what Rosie had told him. She must have had her own reason for putting out so much, but he'd have to think about that later. The name Bill Enright jabbed at him. As far as Harry could recall, Bill wasn't a thug, never really in the Gang, just used for odd cartage jobs. It began to fit together; Arthur would be running not just from the police but from the Gang as well; Harry winced when he thought what the twins would make of Arthur managing to evade capture. And what was that Rosie had said about the safe? It was so heavy that it had made Bill sweat, something like that. Harry's knowledge of safes was extensive; he was able to ease the normal combination versions but he certainly wasn't a patch on Jonathan. But the heavier a safe, the more secure it was. And the heaviest were Champions. Harry sat up with a start. If Arthur's safe was a Champion then perhaps that was what Colin Davies was banging on about. He frowned, thinking he should have put this together sooner. He still had to do something for Jonathan, but what could he say? He didn't know where Arthur was except somewhere in London. He'd have to talk to Colin, well, *Inspector* Davies he thought with a grin.

He telephoned the Society.

Inspector Colin Davies was surprised to hear from Harry; they had been useful to each other in the past, although Colin had been annoyed recently at Harry's flat refusal to tell him where to find the Hare lad. Colin was expecting a change of heart, but Harry had quite another agenda.

"You remember when they rounded up the Grey Gang?" he asked.

Colin mumbled something in agreement.

"Did they catch Arthur Salmon?"

Colin could hardly believe his ears; of course they would have caught Arthur, one of the kingpins wasn't he? But the more he cast his mind back the less certain he was.

He told himself to buy some time.

"What do you mean, Harry?"

"I looked up the papers and didn't see his name. Most of the others, of course; big song and dance put together to suit the Commissioner, weren't it?" asked Harry.

Colin was on dangerous ground. He really ought not to talk to Harry; it hadn't been his operation; that had fallen to Alistair Henderson, and no-one would want to get on his wrong side.

"Tell you what, Harry," he said as positively as he could. "I'll find out for you. Mind you, I'll want something in return." He didn't need to tell Harry what that was.

Alistair Henderson nodded to the duty sergeant and Colin was switched through on that special line. It was odd to get a direct message; he and Colin normally tried to keep a distance between them. After all, Alistair smiled to himself, what Colin did was outside Scotland Yard's jurisdiction and required the practice of some of the 'black arts'.

Colin was businesslike. "Sir, if I were to tell you that we have picked up a rumour concerning Arthur Salmon's whereabouts, would you be interested?"

Alistair grinned; he wasn't going to fall for that old trick.

He had been almost as angry as the Commissioner when Arthur avoided capture. "Breakdown in security somewhere," Sir Hubert had said, looking rather too pointedly at Alistair, but the moment had passed in the general euphoria. So he did indeed want to know where Arthur was.

There was something else, though; there had been some probing by the Sterling Control boys. They were a humourless bunch, City types with horn-rimmed glasses and an air of martyrdom. As far as Alistair could gather, Arthur had been able to get round the controls using a cartel of European Bankers.

"Look, Colin," said Alistair, "let's have lunch. Know anywhere quiet?"

Colin got the message; Alistair was indeed interested but had to keep a distance between them.

Alistair and Colin met in the wine bar that Harry had recommended earlier. The two policemen were in plain clothes by mutual agreement and found the atmosphere particularly suitable.

"Nice place, good choice," said Alistair.

They got plates of food from the bar, Alistair smiling to himself about Colin's glass of wine. He had a beer himself.

"So, Colin, tell me about Arthur."

"My guv'nor wants me to earn my keep," Colin replied with a smile. "I've got to recover some idiot's marker, left it in a new club in Mayfair. Trouble is it's in a Champion safe and I can't find that young man Hare. I can't use an outside mechanic for obvious reasons."

Alistair tried not to move; this was getting too close for comfort. He was beginning to see how brilliantly 'Sir James' had manipulated him. So Colin's only problem was because someone in the upper echelons was pulling strings. The larger question of American penetration of the gambling world wouldn't concern him. But the two were now interwoven.

Alistair waited for Colin to continue, letting him stew for a while.

"I think I can get hold of Mr. Hare if I can locate Arthur Salmon. And I think I can do that with your help."

Alistair smiled bleakly at Colin trying to work a deal. It wasn't an aspect of police work that he normally approved of, but this was too good an opportunity to miss.

"How can I help?" he said neutrally.

"Is it true that Arthur avoided the round up?" Colin tried.

"That's something that the Commissioner would like to keep to himself," Alistair parried, opening the door a crack.

"Look, sir," said Colin, "I know this is your operation but something tells me that Arthur got missed in the sweep. If that's so, I have an opportunity to locate him for you."

Alistair had always thought highly of Colin, not top rank potential perhaps, but sharp enough to be seconded to the Society. Colin had played his hand well so far, and Alistair took a moment to swirl the beer in his glass.

"Fancy finding Caledonian 80/-[28] down here," he said, covering his tracks while he tried to decide what game Colin was playing.

If he had it right, Colin had a reliable tip that might lead to the capture of Arthur. It was a small risk to admit that Arthur was running loose.

"Colin, you've started down a promising avenue and I'd be glad if you'd put any information you can provide into my personal ear," he said with a straight face.

There was a long moment before Colin decided that the superintendent had gone as far as he could. It was clear who'd take the credit if Arthur was recaptured.

Colin telephoned Harry.

"You're going to have to play this very close to your chest, Harry," he said, without preamble.

Harry made appropriate noises.

"The person we spoke about *was* missed."

Harry grinned, thinking that Colin must be on shaky ground to be so artful.

"OK," he responded, "the person is holed up somewhere in the West End. It must be a business handling lots of money and tight security. I think he's got himself an old Champion safe from somewhere, fell off the back of a lorry if I know anything. So there's a young man we both know who you need to persuade to open it. Good luck, I'd say."

"Why's that, Harry?"

"Because the lad knows what was in Arthur's safe and that's a threat Arthur can't live with."

Colin sat quite still. He had been there after the kidnapping when Jonathan had opened the safe, produced a piece of paper and shown it to Sailor. It had been enough to persuade Sailor to rat on the Gang. But what was the threat to Arthur? Sailor had asked how much was in there and

---

28 Caledonian 80/- , brewed in Edinburgh, was Alistair's favourite beer. The qualification 80/- refers to the old method of rating alcohol content, which was taxed by the coinage of the time, the shilling, abbreviated as /-

got the answer 'half a million quid'. Colin had assumed it was the Gang's money but now that he thought about the way Sailor had reacted, Arthur must have been siphoning it off; the Gang would never forgive him and it was enough to get him killed. If Arthur could get his hands on Hare, there might be another body floating in the Thames.

"Another thing," said Harry, speaking slowly, "I think there's a tail on the young expert at his humble abode, sounds like someone from Dockland, not very good at it, but will be reporting back; if we can deal with that then perhaps we can get some cooperation."

Colin thought that over. An operation to neutralise the tail would have to come from Alistair's Division; he was sure that would be possible.

"We'll deal with the tail, Harry," he said confidently. "Where's Mr. Hare?"

Harry laughed, "Not so fast, Inspector, I've got some knitting to do."

Colin put down the telephone, thinking that he could just see a glimmer of hope that he could get the marker back. Like Harry, though, he had some loose ends to tie up.

NINE

Where there's Smoke

JONATHAN WAS EXAMINING THE OFFICIAL CALENDAR THAT indicated that the first function of the Michaelmas Term required him to wear a dinner jacket, so he asked the tailors to finish it ahead of the rest of his wardrobe. He grinned at the thought of having a range of clothes that he could call a 'wardrobe'.

When he woke the next morning he made breakfast for himself and ate it bachelor-style, scrambled eggs out of the pan, standing up and looking out of the window. He nearly choked when he saw Hilary sailing across the quad. She was on her way up. He rushed about and was decent when she knocked.

She stood on the mat. "May I come in?"

Jonathan was amazed at her new deference. "Of course, Hilary, I'm glad you came."

She walked carefully away from him, and sat in one of the low chairs, not meeting his eyes.

He offered her some tea, but she shook her head.

She was swinging one of her promising legs again.

"You don't mind me being here after, well, after what happened last time?"

"You took me by surprise; I thought it was the man who should be the first to make a move."

She was angry now. "So you belong to that old school, do you?"

Jonathan was stumped once more. "What do you mean?"

"Well, if a girl fancies a man, why shouldn't she let him know?"

Jonathan had no idea how to answer. "It's just that all the girls I know are, um, a bit 'old school' themselves."

A change had come over Hilary.

She got up abruptly. "Yes," she muttered, "I bet they are!" and before he could react, she had gone out and slammed the door. Once more, he was lost in the jungle of feminine behaviour.

Superintendent Alistair Henderson's rapid promotion was due in part to what the Scots like to call 'canniness'[29]. Colin's offer to locate Arthur was at least one stage from assured, otherwise he would have used the phrase 'I know where he is'. A successful operation to combine the eradication of the American threat and the capture of Arthur would be a coup. But as things stood there was no evidence that Arthur was holed up in the Club. Lots of circumstantial stuff, he mused, more than Colin would know about certainly. But not enough to go before a magistrate for a search warrant, he knew that. So he'd have to tie Arthur to the club. Then he could use the Sterling Control boys to push the right buttons, raid the club and find something illegal enough to shut it down.

Harry telephoned Jonathan and more or less invited himself down to Oxford. Jonathan knew Harry hated leaving the Smoke so there had to be something important involved. He was glad Harry was coming, but realised with a shock that he must be in some sort of danger.

Colin Davies met Alistair at a pub in Woolwich, not that far from the Society. It was a huge establishment on a corner of the Town Square, all brass and frosted windows. It was a working man's pub so they went into the saloon bar away from the thundering noise of thirsty dockers and warehousemen drinking and shouting lewd comments across the room. Colin thought Alistair was looking a bit pale around the gills.

---

29   To the Scots this means 'shrewd' or 'far-sighted'; other meanings are less complimentary.

When they were settled with Colin nursing an IPA[30] rather than wine, he said, "My expert is in danger, sir, from the person we are both interested in. We'll need to protect him."

Alistair stared into his glass; he realised that he could dangle the 'expert' under Arthur's nose and follow the trail; then he could get Arthur for kidnapping and assault. He could see Colin's point of view, but the lad was too valuable as bait. For the plan to work, Arthur must make his move, and providing protection might dissuade him. It was a neat and economical plan that appealed to his innate frugality.

Alistair made all the right noises to Colin; he had a team in mind, he said; it had a great record, even been used by the Intelligence Services, he hinted.

Sir James would have been surprised by that claim.

Alistair had another thought; he still hadn't met the young man, something he would have to put right.

Jonathan's telephone rang.

"Mr. Hare, sir," announced Jason, "there is a person at the Lodge asking for you."

It was obvious from the emphasis on the word 'person' that Jason disapproved.

Harry must have arrived. Jonathan couldn't help smiling at the comparison between the two men. Jason was all Queen and Country, while Harry was an example of the segment of the population that had been sneered at during the years after the War, what did they call them, 'spivs' and 'wide boys', that was it.

"I'll come down, Jason."

To his amazement he found Harry in Jason's inner room, drinking tea out of an enamel mug of massive dimensions.

When Harry saw him he got up quickly and tapped the side of his nose, which Jonathan knew was Harry's way of saying 'shtumm'. To Jonathan's surprise, Jason winked.

---

30   India Pale Ale, a brew designed to assuage the thirst of the British in India.

Harry took Jonathan's elbow. "Let's see your Rooms, then," he said.

But as soon as they were in the open, he started to manhandle Jonathan away from the Lodge. It was as physical as Harry had ever been and Jonathan protested.

When they were safely upstairs, Harry said, "You should've picked up on that bit of stagecraft, mate."

Jonathan smiled, "For the sake of the watcher?"

Harry scowled, "Too smart for your own boots, ain't yer?"

"Look," he continued, "we've got to pull one over old donkey jacket so he can't tip Arthur the wink."

"Who's 'we'," asked Jonathan, keeping his face straight.

Harry looked sharply at him.

"You might as well know; me and Bill Jason go back a bit. He was stationed in London just after the War, Guard duty at the Tower. I helped him out once or twice; those squaddies[31] of his could get into real trouble. He didn't recognise me at first, what a giggle!"

Jonathan took a moment to look more carefully at Harry. He wasn't wearing the padded shoulders and loud tie that he had when Jonathan worked with him in London. In fact Harry had adopted a style of dress that made him almost invisible, Harris Tweed jacket and grey flannel trousers just like any ordinary chap in a provincial town like Oxford. Nice bit of camouflage, thought Jonathan.

Harry looked around the Rooms, nodding with approval. "They must think a lot of you; bet you like it here. Got clout too," he said, nodding towards the telephone[32].

After Harry completed his inspection he went to look out of the window over the Quadrangle.

Without turning he said, "Look, mate, we're pretty sure Arthur's behind this. I reckon you're safe here, Arthur wouldn't try anything this

---

31 Military slang for private soldiers, or in this case, Guardsmen.
32   It was impossible to get a telephone installed quickly unless you knew the sort of people that Harry knew.

far from the Smoke. We need more time to find where Arthur's holed up. Now that I know Bill's here, you're more than safe. Keep your head down, phone me if you need to."

And with that he went out the door with a grin and a wave.

Jonathan sat down feeling a bit more relaxed. Harry would want to be back in the Smoke, certainly by the time the pubs opened.

Jonathan's telephone rang; Jason said, "There is a Superintendent Henderson on the line, Mr. Hare sir, he says he's a friend of Inspector Colin Davies."

Jonathan's immediate thought was that someone was putting more pressure on him to open that safe, so he said, "Could you tell him I'm out, Jason?"

But Jason was ahead of the game. He had surprised Alistair by asking a number of penetrating questions. When Alistair tried to object, Jason had said with an authority that Alistair had to admire, "Mr. Hare is the Galdraith Scholar, sir, and my personal responsibility."

"I think you should speak with the superintendent, sir," said Jason, "he has some important news for you."

When Alistair was connected he said, "We haven't met, Mr. Hare, but I've heard some good things about you from Inspector Davies. If I understand it, you believe you're in some sort of danger from a person in whom I have an interest."

Jonathan made the correct noises.

"Would it be helpful if I provided some protection against this person?"

Jonathan agreed.

"In that case I shall send down a team. You won't see them; they will liaise with your Head Porter, who is already aware of the plan. You should be thankful to have such an excellent man watching out for you. Oh, one more thing," said Alistair nonchalantly, "I would like to brief you personally on our plan. Perhaps in due time you can come up to the Yard? With the team of course," he added smoothly.

Encouraged by the superintendent's concern Jonathan was feeling less threatened, so he agreed.

The report on the Scholar that Jason presented to Lord Galdraith came as a shock. His Scholar was involved in some serious matter arising from the rounding up of the Grey Gang. Jonathan had got the wrong side of one of the Gang who had evaded capture. Senior police officers were involved. Jason considered that Mr. Hare was an innocent party in need of protection. Lord Galdraith shouldn't be surprised if an undercover police team was assigned.

William thought about Jason's report for a moment or two. Jason couldn't be aware of the content of the disgraceful document foisted onto the Selection Committee. He thanked Jason for the information and was reassured when Jason remarked that there was no immediate threat and that he had already put certain measures in place.

Alistair decided on the team he would use to bring Jonathan to London. Two would be enough and they'd have to recognize the young man. Charmaine Montpelier was an obvious candidate, and Sergeant Dobson had been the barman in the 'King's Head' when Ronnie was captured. They could pass as a couple.

He smiled as he recalled that he had promised the team would watch Jonathan's back in Oxford, but that would have defeated the plan. He had to get Hare into London; Arthur Salmon wouldn't be tempted anywhere else. Briefing the team would take some guile; if he let them into the plan it would compromise their behaviour.

Sergeant Dobson was ready and willing, but Charmaine was surprisingly resistant. He would have to be more discreet; she was, after all, on exchange from the French Sécurité.

"Look, Miss Montpelier, I must have someone who is close to the young man and I know you had that task during the Grey operation."

He was surprised to see the young woman blushing and she was shifting uncomfortably in her chair.

"Sir, is this an order?"

Her chin was thrust forward.

Alistair sat back and looked at her. He needed willing cooperation.

"You have a problem?" he said with a smile of encouragement.

"I did get close to him, just part of my job, sir," she said hurriedly, "but he's just too young to be mixed up in something like this."

It was Alistair's turn to be taken aback.

"What do you mean, 'something like this'?"

There was an awkward silence.

"He's so naïve, sir, and yet the Commissioner made him out to be a member of the Gang."

She stopped, chewing her lip. Alistair could tell she was going to say something else.

"He's a civilian, not in the Force."

Alistair waited, although he was getting the feeling that something was about to be revealed.

She sat up straight in her chair.

"There's a rumour, sir, that he was used improperly in the operation to catch the Gang."

Alistair was shocked. "Miss Montpelier, that is a dangerous allegation. The young man was kidnapped by the Gang and we followed them to the warehouse."

Charmaine had gone quite white. "Sir, what I understand from the cafeteria chat is that the Yard knew all along that the Gang would snatch the young man, otherwise arrangements couldn't have been made in advance like the team watching the Gang's Watford depot."

Alistair was stunned; there was no way to refute that. He thought back to the Commissioner smiling when he said that C division would handle any intercepts allowing Alistair to concentrate on the warehouse. The failure of the intercept at Watford had come through the grapevine but it had all been in the noise as far as Alistair was concerned.

If what Charmaine had heard was true it put a whole new slant on the operation, and not one he liked at all. But he mustn't give anything away.

He stared at Charmaine and said, "I'm surprised at you, Miss Montpelier, listening to such gossip. It's true that young Hare was in some danger for a while and if we'd got our hands on all the Gang members this operation wouldn't be necessary. But one of them escaped and is threatening the young man. So your cooperation is essential to prevent any unfortunate repercussions."

"You mean Arthur Salmon is threatening Jonathan?" she asked. Alistair realized that the Yard grapevine wouldn't have missed the fact that Arthur hadn't been among those captured; and he noted that she had used Hare's first name. So he would use that as leverage.

"Yes, and Arthur will think that the young man was working for us. Of course, that's rubbish, but if he thinks so, vengeance will be top of his agenda, won't it?"

Charmaine nodded, thinking that perhaps she should stay with this operation after all. Something didn't sit right with her. Call it a woman's intuition if you like, but the superintendent had sent some strange signals, taking just a bit too long to digest what she'd said.

"Sir, perhaps I was a bit hasty. Since I do know him pretty well, I'll take on the job."

All Alistair could do was smile, hoping it was his personal charm that had done the trick.

The next day the tailors' shop telephoned Jonathan to say that his dinner jacket was ready and would he please attend for the final fitting. He went downstairs and walked past the Porter's Lodge. As he did so Jason said, rather too loudly Jonathan thought, "Good afternoon, Mr Hare, sir." Jonathan looked across the road and saw that the donkey jacket was still in the book shop, so he decided it was safe to walk to the tailors. The police team promised by the superintendent would watch his back. The superintendent had said that he wouldn't see them.

What Jonathan might have seen was a man in a blue uniform walking casually on the other side of the street. In Oxford he was invisible, just another porter going off duty.

The fitting for his dinner jacket went uneventfully and Jonathan enjoyed his walk back to Abingdon College, thinking that the police team must be good, he hadn't seen anything unusual.

Arthur Salmon had been receiving regular reports from the tail he had sent to Oxford. He was getting frustrated; surely that fink Hare would get out of Oxford one day so he could get his hands on him. He didn't have much time because Joe had reminded him recently that Hare was still his problem. Unless he took care of it soon, Joe had hinted, he would send some muscle down to Oxford himself. Arthur was worried about using measures that might work in the States, but would be unforgivable over here. He had started to advise Joe that anything like that and the rozzers wouldn't rest until they got a collar. But one look at Joe's face had convinced Arthur that discretion was the better part of valour. What Arthur didn't tell Joe was that Hare seemed to have some sort of protection in place.

The tail had reported, "Target never leaves the college without a porter in sight. They all look as if they can take care of themselves."

Had the tail known that Jason had recruited his porters from a list of retired Coldstream Guardsmen he might have given Arthur even more food for thought.

Sir Roger and his brother met in an emergency session to deal with the failure to discredit the Hare fellow at the Galdraith interview. Sir Hubert detected some signs of stress and concern in his brother; most unusual, he couldn't remember Roger ever being anything but cool and unflappable. Hubert had already justified to himself that the end result of their plot had far outweighed the hazards, and the dummy document that Roger had used was easily explained away as a mistake by a bumbling low level clerk, obviously never taken seriously, there was no DPS number, was there?

So why was Roger so unsettled? Did he have something else on his conscience? Hubert had kept himself entirely out of Roger's efforts to protect the Bellestreams, and if Roger had taken any other steps against Hare, well, that was his affair.

Hubert vaguely recalled some half-baked idea that Hare and Victoria were getting too close; preposterous really, but if Antonia had got her teeth into that idea, she might have imposed her famously selfish demands and Roger might have done something to break up the relationship simply to pacify Antonia.

Hubert shrugged; it was none of his business, so he rejected any of Roger's pathetic ideas designed to distance them from any consequences. Let Roger suffer a bit, wouldn't do him any harm.

But there Sir Hubert was wrong.

Ten

Vengeance is Mine

In 1928 Kurt Weill was living in America when he wrote a song called 'Pirate Jenny'. It should have served as a warning to the American people, especially Southerners; it depicted such a thirst for revenge that no one should have been surprised when, forty years later, America exploded with black activism. In the context of this song the 1968 race riots in Watts were entirely predictable.

The song tells of a black servant girl in a Southern seaport hotel, looked down upon by the residents and condemned to a life of drudgery, cleaning and scrubbing after them. She dreams that she is a pirate and her ship, the black freighter, pulls into that port and blasts the hotel to the ground. All those left alive are brought to <u>her</u> for a decision and she tells the pirates to 'kill them, kill them all'. As the bodies pile up, she croaks (and the black singer Nina Simone was the most ardent expositor), 'That'll learn ya!'

When Colin returned to the Society there was an unusually terse note from Sir Roger demanding to know what progress he had made in retrieving the marker. The 'engaged' light above the private door into Sir Roger's study was not on, so Colin knocked and waited. He could hear something from the room, but there was no 'come in', just a low moan.

He opened the door and saw Sir Roger slumped over the desk, the usual gin and tonic glass overturned and dribbling its contents over some papers. He rushed in and, after one look, picked up the telephone.

"Ambulance, no bells, no lights!" He gave the address and a codeword.

He got Sir Roger onto the floor, opened his collar and checked that he hadn't swallowed his tongue. Pulse seemed fine, he thought, but breathing not right. He propped the guv's head up with a cushion and went quickly to the main door to the study and set the internal lock; he couldn't have anyone see the guv like this. Nothing to be done, he thought, but hope that bloody ambulance gets here soon.

Jonathan remembered that he had promised to telephone Victoria. Thomas answered, and sounded less smooth than usual.

"Miss Victoria has gone to London, sir; Sir Roger has been taken ill, had to be admitted. Sergeant, excuse me, sir, *Inspector* Davies may have saved his life. Perhaps I could take a message for Miss Victoria?"

Jonathan was shaken, and told Thomas that he would try to contact her, "At the Society, Thomas?" Thomas agreed.

When he got through, he heard the steady tones of Colin Davies. Jonathan and he had shared several excitements, including a fast drive to York Station across the moors. Jonathan had never been so scared but was determined not to show it. And they had worked together getting Jane out of danger and capturing Sailor and Freddy. Jonathan had never felt that Colin had anything to do with how Sir Roger had treated him afterwards.

Colin was thanking his stars that Jonathan had rung; it was decent of him; he wondered how he had found out? Before he could ask where Jonathan was, he sensed Miss Victoria reaching for the phone. It was unlike her to be pushy, so he handed it over, trying to signal to her that he needed to talk too.

"Jonathan, is that you?" she said, out of breath. "My father is in a hospital; can't find mother anywhere, apparently she went off in a temper, she took a *taxi* from here. We are all shocked, of course."

For a moment, he thought they were shocked that Lady Antonia had stooped to take a taxi, but recovered in time to ask, "Is there anything I can do?"

She hesitated, and then said, "Not at the moment, Jonathan, Inspector Davies is here. But it means a lot to me that you called."

Lady Antonia de Quincy was sitting in the lounge of an entirely private club in Belgravia. She had had no trouble getting the taxi driver to take an enormous tip to forget to radio in. Her temper had subsided a bit, but her fury at Roger had drained her. She was clutching a gin and tonic, glad to have even that tiny serving; it wouldn't drown a mouse, she had to plead for more ice as though it was rationed or something. She had garnered the usual looks from some men in the other bar, and treated them to some words that she had almost forgotten were in her repertoire. The men, worldly though they were, had rocked back in amazement.

She wondered whether he would come; it was a long shot, but what else could she do; to hell with Roger, stuck up ponce, and Victoria, well, she could go her own way, if she wouldn't listen to her, then let her suffer the way *she* had. Almost unconsciously, she raised the back of her hand to her brow; it might have looked good in an Edwardian melodrama, but her present audience assumed she must be perspiring.

The door opened and in walked Rudolph behind another man larger than anyone else in the club. There was a general exodus, with the servants looking nervous; even the manager appeared and grovelled a bit.

"Elaine?" Rudolph asked, hardly able to believe his eyes.

"Hello, Rudolf," she said icily, using the name they had chosen all those years ago.

The chief executive of the Bessemer movement had been thinking about the assets that Hare had retrieved from Mountbeck. In fact, he had been unable to get them out of his mind. He had educated himself in the technicalities of Bearer Bonds, and had had no difficulty imagining what he could do with the money. The movement had plenty of funds tied up in all sorts of bequests, each controlled by trusts and only useful after Board meetings and approval of trustees. He recalled several major acquisitions that had nearly come to grief when it had taken so long to release the funds.

But this was a different proposition. It was obscene that one family could sit on liquid assets of this magnitude, and it was obviously a device to avoid income tax on the interest. Probably not subject to Death Duties either, untraceable by definition. He made a decision – spot of holidays in the Scilly Isles, Cornish Riviera Express to Penzance, just a short boat trip from there.

When he arrived in the Isles, he scouted out Old Town and found the Bank. He barged in and slammed the briefcase onto the counter. The manager hurried forward and ushered him into a small office. The big man shoved the bonds towards the manager.

"Like to cash these, soon as possible, if you please," he said in that commanding North Country voice that could terrify the most experienced solicitors and City bank directors. It had never entered his mind that the Bank might not hold so much cash. He was used to seeing nervousness, rather happy to see it, actually; it gave him leverage, so he didn't see anything unusual about the sweat beading the manager's forehead.

The manager cleared his throat, "It will take a day or two to meet all of these, sir. I can help you with a small amount immediately, but, well, it's not every day we see quite this volume of business."

The huge man drummed his fingers, and then decided, "Staying at the 'Harbour Inn'; ring me there."

When he had left the office, the manager, still sweating, set in motion a plan spelled out in a document he was under strict instructions to keep in his safe.

Lady Antonia and Rudolf had taken a remote corner of the room. Almost without a word, the other members had moved away, the presence of the bodyguard being sufficient encouragement. She was consumed with anger that both her daughter and Roger had thwarted her. That Sir Roger might have met her demands eventually had no interest for her; she was used to instant gratification and determined that those who got in her way should pay the price.

The arrangement she proposed might have unsettled someone less worldly than Rudolph; she had no intention of keeping her side of the bargain, she just wanted to give Roger something to think about the next time he chose to oppose her.

Far away in the Scilly Isles, messages had been flashing to and fro. The manager had been given his instructions. A team of plainclothes police from the Yard had been dispatched, and would arrive the next day.

Rudolf was trying to get his thoughts together. He had imagined that dalliances such as she had suggested were things of history. More sinister thoughts followed immediately. Imagine that bastard Roger sending his wife to entrap him; what a way to behave. Then the full brilliance of the offer hit him. He had to sit down. He ordered drinks for them, snarling something about the size of the portions at the steward, who turned white and hurried away. He was so stunned that he couldn't speak for a while. She had built a web for him and he was caught; whichever path he chose he was going to suffer. He just hoped that he could keep it from the press. 'Hell hath no fury' he quoted to himself, only too aware of how well it applied.

Back in the Scilly Isles, the chief executive had at last remembered the caution recommended by the Headmaster. Was it possible that Hare had knowingly delivered bogus assets? He was sure that the lad, for all his special expertise, had no counterfeiting skills, nothing in his file, certainly.

He replayed the conversation at St. Eligius. The Headmaster had said something to the effect that Hare might have been 'suborned by a government service'. If that was true, then they could have had fake documents prepared. He recalled also that the negotiations with Mountbeck over the

Abercorn property had run into another brick wall; he'd assumed that the family would be even more anxious to sell.

He had fought his way through trade union ranks, which were just as political and cut-throat as any other bureaucratic quagmire, with a native astuteness. He thought of the timing; he had deposited the bonds just yesterday so time was on his side. He decided to have a cup of tea at the tiny airport, book a ticket, just in case.

When he got there, he checked the incoming flights, written in chalk on a blackboard. There was a flight from Bristol due any time. He got his tea; it was pathetically weak; it wouldn't be used to wash dishes anywhere along the Tyne, where they'd call it 'maiden's water'.

A small aircraft dropped out of the sky and taxied towards the terminal. A set of steps was wheeled up and pushed against the side of the plane. He watched as several women came excitedly down, followed by a group of men who might have been rugby players, except that they carried with them that special aura that he recognised immediately. They were policemen, he was sure of that, five of them, typical heavy squad after a prime suspect. He thought about his own position; he had a receipt from the bank manager, using one of his many identities; 'can't ever be too careful, eh lad?' as his father had always said.

So, he thought, if I just leave the bonds here, and this trap isn't what I think it is, I could get at them later. He patted the ticket in his pocket; his plane left in an hour.

Lady Antonia was pleasantly surprised that Rudolf had swallowed the bait. It wasn't much to ask, and the reward as enticing as she could make it. She had no comprehension of the dilemma she had created, nor would she have cared had she known.

A phrase from her East End childhood swam into her mind 'That'll learn ya!' she thought, in expectation of the joy that she would experience when she saw Roger's reaction. "Never speak to me that way again, will he?"

Sir Roger de Quincy was emerging from his coma. He wondered if he was already dead; everything was white and pristine, so white that it hurt his eyes. When he had recovered more fully, he found that his wrists were restrained, tubes were attached to his body and instruments were making rhythmic noises.

So, he thought, God has not taken me yet.

A nurse appeared, mouthing the time-honoured phrase, "Ah, you're awake, then!"

He responded, as all do apparently, "Where am I?"

The nurse, so scrupulously and expensively trained, had a ready answer, "The doctor will be here in just a few moments."

His memory was flooding back. He had himself approved the Standing Orders for Duty Officers that every DO had to read first thing on watch. Section XIV dealt with the serious incapacity of senior officers. He would have been transported anonymously to the sanatorium, maintained at such expense, but necessary to contain the more serious emergencies affecting those in the hierarchy.

The doctor arrived and conducted a series of checks.

"Well, Sir Roger, I'm glad to have you back with us; touch and go for a while, there. No physical damage as far as I can see. But that's not to discount other difficulties. You will need to rest here for some while. No return to duties until I can get clearance from above."

For a moment, Roger fantasized that the doctor would require Heavenly permission. Then he remembered that in his case the procedures called for a special authority that could only be granted by one person. He started to protest but found it difficult in wrist straps. The doctor would not remove them, explaining that, such was the body's reaction to his condition, with adrenalin flow greatly amplified in volume and immediacy, he could damage himself, or others.

"Some patients hurl themselves right out of bed, Sir Roger; no one can explain it; something like an earthquake, release of stored-up tension in that moment when the structure can contain it no longer. We can all cope up to a point, but we also have finite capacities. We think that you have simply reached that threshold."

Roger took some of this in. The doctor opined that 'the only remedy is rest and relaxation, time the great healer', and departed.

He dozed and dreamed that he was a boy again, in danger and nobody cared, everyone looking away from him, while a pack of dogs was at his heels. Somehow he escaped and ran to his father for comfort, but his father turned his back, opening a door that led downwards, ever downwards. A woman appeared, one in his debt, who reached out and pushed him down the stairs. He was falling, lashing out at everyone and hitting no one.

When he came round, the nurse was trying to calm him.

ELEVEN

Vested Interests

COLIN WAS CALLED TO A MEETING OF the Management Committee of the Society where he was told that the recovery of the marker was an operational matter and, in Sir Roger's temporary absence, he was to assume responsibility for the file. He left the meeting thinking that they'd found a convenient way to avoid the uproar if things went wrong.

He took over Sir Roger's office and began to read the Royal Person's file. It had been savagely annotated in a manner quite foreign to Sir Roger's usually immaculate style. When he got to the page noting the information about the safe, Sir Roger's pencil had ripped right through the paper, so much so that Colin could hardly read the word 'Champion'. It was followed by the single word 'Hare' that Sir Roger had pencilled over a number of times, the letters now thick and heavy. Colin could make no sense of it until he recalled Harry's strange burst of temper. Young Hare must have really got on the wrong side of Sir Roger.

He looked around for the Hare file but couldn't find it, so he called in the Chief Clerk who pursed her lips and clutched at her Ciro[33] pearls.

"I am sorry, Inspector," she murmured, "but that file has been logged out to Sir Roger personally. I haven't seen it for some time now."

She stood there looking worried.

---

33 Ciro *faux* pearls were famous for their quality. Professional middle-class women frequently wore a twin set and pearls at work, almost like a uniform.

Colin realised that she had more to say, so he said, "I'm not blaming anyone, but surely it can't be unavailable?"

"I'm afraid it is, sir," she said and rushed on, "but if I may say so, that file seemed to be of great concern to Sir Roger. In fact I have seen him, well, lock it in his briefcase."

This was a particularly improper procedure; Colin knew that removing a file would be grounds for dismissal. Be that as it may, he had to accept that the Hare file was not available to him.

He sat back and thought about Jonathan Hare; he remembered the peculiar behaviour of Miss Victoria when the young man had telephoned. She had reached for the handset with an urgency that was quite out of keeping. He had only heard her side of it, but her words reflected a degree of friendship that had taken him by surprise. The young man had obviously offered his help and she had said something like "Not right now" as if she could call on his assistance at any time. He shook his head; perhaps the de Quincys had been afraid that she was infatuated with him. And if Lady Antonia had seized on that idea, it would explain a lot.

He wondered if Miss Victoria might know where Hare was; he went looking for her.

"Abingdon College, I think," she had said distractedly, "anyway it's in Oxford where he won the Scholarship."

That information would have been in the Hare file had it not been spirited away. He could have kicked himself; if he had paid more attention to the gossip at Mountbeck he would have known about the Scholarship. But his orders had been clear; keep the Movement away from the lad while he opened the Bellestream safe. Everything else had seemed unimportant, and now he had new orders; the marker had to be recovered and for that he needed Hare. A trip to Oxford was essential, but he would find it hard to get away from the Society. Miss Victoria was so upset and he had to keep a lid on the situation, for he couldn't allow her to discover the reason for her father's attack. And he couldn't tell her where her father was either; the sanatorium was a secret and her father was there because his position made it mandatory.

Colin decided to use Sir Roger's privileges and asked the Society's switchboard operator to find a contact number at Abingdon College in Oxford. When the telephone rang the operator said, "The Porter's Lodge is the best I can do, sir; I have a Mr. Jason on the line."

But Jason was as protective as Harry and Travis and the only thing Colin could do was to leave his name and number, adding 'at the Society'. What had Jason said? Something like, "I shall tell Mr. Hare that you called, Mr. Davies."

It was almost as if young Hare was in need of protection, and that would explain a lot. But the urgency surrounding the marker remained, so he would have to resort to more direct means and get himself down to Oxford.

The man known occasionally as 'Sir James' had received confirmation from Alistair that the lease of the Club in South Audley Street had changed hands in a manner certainly not approved by Westminster Holdings, the Duke of Westminster's operating company. Alistair had made other enquiries and discovered that the previous tenant had disappeared, whereabouts currently unknown, and had signed over the lease to the present incumbents. When the leasing agent saw the extent of the alterations and the obvious intent, he was furious and wanted to close them down immediately. Alistair had to exert all his authority to prevent a catastrophe by agreeing to come up with a solution within forty-eight hours.

"Better be good, superintendent," the agent had said, "or they'll have my guts for garters."

Jason was thinking about Mr. Jonathan Hare. Lord Galdraith had made it clear during the preparations for the Interview that he was to 'keep an eye out for him'. But fancy the Committee selecting Mr. Hare – such a proper candidate, turned himself out smartly in an officer's suit and what looked like a regimental tie. He carried himself with that special attitude that he had seen so often at Sandhurst. It sets a man apart, but Mr. Hare didn't have that snobbishness that some of them had; they were stuck-up ponces, their 'daddy' solving all their problems for them, with more money than sense. Their Army career would be just a pastime for them, he thought bitterly.

Many would serve a few years then go into the family business, with a job already theirs; they would jump over hardworking career men, wouldn't they? Some would get their names in the newspapers, caught with their hand in the till.

But they were the exceptions; he was immensely proud of those cadets in his Company that had done well; not that they had to go through anything like the War, but it was best not to dwell on that, it might get his blood pressure up.

It had been hard to step away from his army career; with all that companionship and a language all their own, it was like being in a huge club. He smiled at the way he had got this job; Major Beauchamp had been so persuasive. There was an officer for you, he stood no nonsense but really cared about his men.

"Job might have been designed for you, Sergeant Major, they're lucky to get you; new College like that needs some discipline; keep those young people in hand, what?"

Jason had saluted with extra zeal and nearly buckled the peak of his hat, hadn't he?

And then he had discovered that his so-called retirement had another aspect to it; he was to lend his services to the Officer Training Corps. Even if they'd changed the name, it was still, in his mind, the way to pick out officer material from the undergraduates.

Colin decided that he would take Victoria with him to Oxford so she couldn't pick up any improper information at the Society. Only yesterday he had overheard one of the staff muttering about 'gin and tonics at ten thirty in the morning'; he had dealt out a stern warning, but the knowledge was in play and who knew what Victoria might overhear? She was popular with the staff, a nice young woman who had been raised to treat people properly. And her recent tragedy with that young Scotsman, Lord something or other, had made the staff even more sympathetic to her.

Her reaction when he proposed the trip confirmed his earlier thoughts about her relationship with Hare. Her face brightened and she rushed upstairs to get her things. He got Martin to bring round the Rolls Royce and they crossed London using small roads known to police and emergency services as the only way to make any time. Colin wondered whether the authorities would ever do anything about the South Circular Road, a real bottleneck, especially from Greenwich. Eventually they were through the great city and speeding up the A 40 admiring the view of Oxford as they approached.

"City of Dreaming Spires," Victoria said almost to herself.

Jason intercepted them at the Porter's Lodge with an authority that Colin had to admire. They were told that Jason would see if 'the Scholar is in his Rooms'. Meanwhile, they should please wait right here in the reception area.

When Jonathan picked up the telephone, Jason announced that the same large motor car was at the Lodge and that he had two visitors. Jonathan was taken aback; surely it couldn't be Sir Roger?

"Did they give their names, Jason?"

There was a muted conversation. "Your visitors are Miss Victoria and *Inspector* Colin Davies, Mr. Hare, sir."

Jonathan's relief found its way into his response. "Oh, I'll be right down, Jason."

Victoria held out both hands towards him, something she had never done before. He was initially taken aback but realized that this was a prelude to a hug. He felt Victoria press her cheek against his; it felt good and he caught a tiny fragrance of the perfume that he remembered from her letters.

Colin stood to one side, noticing another demonstration of affection, although the young man didn't appear as enthusiastic as Victoria.

"Inspector Davies wants to talk to you, Jonathan," she said, "so I decided to come too. Perhaps we could have that afternoon tea that you promised me?"

Jonathan had to laugh, recalling that impromptu invitation when they were up at the White Horse. He was about to suggest the 'Kardoma' when Victoria said, "Why don't we go to the 'Randolph'? We went there quite often when I was at Oxenham."

Jonathan felt a bit uneasy; the Randolph Hotel was the most luxurious in Oxford and beyond the imagination of a young lad on a bike. He had been past it many times, hard to miss really, since it was almost in the middle of the City. But then, he remembered, he had managed the Savoy in London, and after that, any hotel would be quite ordinary. And so it proved, although arriving in a chauffeur-driven Rolls Royce made sure that they were received as honoured guests. Victoria seemed quite at home and greeted the head waiter by name.

He bowed discreetly, "How very nice to see you again, Miss Victoria, we haven't seen enough of you since you left Oxenham."

Jonathan smiled to himself; it was as if Victoria was part of a huge family always welcome in the very best places. He thought he could get used to it.

Lady Hecate had heard from her contact in Northumberland Avenue; she knew him by quite another name than 'Sir James'. He was sure she understood that it would be more than inappropriate for him to intercede directly but she should expect a telephone call from a Superintendent Henderson.

Sir James outlined the present difficulty with the Grosvenor agent.

"Perhaps a word in the proper ear, what?" he said jovially, adding, "on the other matter, inopportune actions should be avoided. National interest at play here, don't you know?"

She realised that her son's peccadillo would have to take a lower priority. She sighed, thinking that perhaps it would do him no harm to sweat a bit.

Whether there were any family connections between Lady Hecate's line and the Grosvenor family was rather beside the point. People in that exalted stratum knew each other as a result of countless social and charitable functions that they graced with their presence. Their children may have attended the same schools, done the Season together and been married in the same fashionable churches. So Lady Hecate's telephone call was swiftly connected to the member of the family on the Management Board. He was of a military persuasion and jumped at the chance to get some real action. The agent that Alistair had spoken with was astonished to receive direct orders from the Board member. He left the meeting thinking that he had seriously underestimated the superintendent's authority.

Victoria excused herself, muttering about "powdering her nose", with a meaningful glance at Colin. Jonathan knew what was coming and braced himself. Colin had decided to go out on a limb; there was no use having power if you didn't use it.

"Look, Mr. Hare, I know you and Sir Roger have had some sort of falling out, but he'll be away for a while, no chance of you running into him again. So it's me that's asking for your help; there's a lot riding on this for me, even my promotion."

Jonathan heard the phrase 'be away for a while' and wondered what Colin meant.

"Is Sir Roger ill?" he asked, putting Colin on the spot.

"Let's just say that he has other interests that will occupy him exclusively for some time."

Jonathan thought that must be some sort of police code, but he trusted Colin enough to accept the explanation.

Colin dived in, "I have to retrieve this marker from a Club in Mayfair." He saw Jonathan's frown.

"It's an IOU, Mr. Hare, but it was left by, shall we say, a person of great importance. The club is playing hard to get and they keep all that sort of stuff in a safe."

Jonathan held up his hand. "It's a Champion, isn't it?"

Colin realised that Jonathan was a step ahead, but wasn't prepared for the next outburst.

"Look, Inspector, I'm the Galdraith Scholar, I'm not going to risk that."

And the more Colin pressed him, the more Jonathan resisted. Colin was having a difficult time finding new arguments until Jonathan's anger burst forth.

"Don't you remember the last time I helped by opening a Champion safe? Your boss and the Commissioner turned against me; it nearly cost me this Scholarship!"

Colin's astonishment was written plainly on his face. But then he understood what Harry had been saying; the blame wasn't down to Jonathan, but to Sir Roger. What had Harry said? That it was Sir Roger who had 'crapped in his corner', that was it.

He was trying hard to think of something to counter Jonathan's outburst when Victoria returned.

"And did you have a good chat?" she asked them sweetly.

There wasn't much that Colin could do after that and they took Jonathan back to the College.

Colin and Victoria got in the car and left for the Society. He was unusually silent and Victoria's persistent questions about Jonathan began to irritate him.

"You and Jonathan had an argument, didn't you?" she asked, "I know that look; he can be, well, forceful when he wants. I bet he refused to do whatever you wanted of him."

Colin was unnerved, for this was far too close to the truth.

"Yes, Miss Victoria," he said. "I wasn't able to persuade him. He's very focussed on this Scholarship, isn't he?"

Victoria nodded. "Well, he doesn't have anything else to fall back on, you know. My father told me that Jonathan was being groomed to succeed him, and that he would mentor him, but something went wrong. Jonathan is angry at my father, but I don't know why. Do you know?"

Colin was sure that he would have known about something as fundamental to the Society as a decision to prepare for Sir Roger's replacement. Perhaps it was something that Sir Roger had used as a smokescreen to deflect Victoria's interest in the lad. But he had to answer.

"Well, I don't know exactly, Miss Victoria, but it does seem that your father and Mr. Hare have had some sort of disagreement, a falling out, perhaps."

"I think it must be more than that," was all Victoria would say, with sadness in her voice. Colin noted another sign of concern. And, he thought, what had the lad meant when he said he'd nearly lost the Scholarship? They were nearly back at the Society before he recalled that Reggie Forsyth, pompous idiot, had retired and had taken a position at Oxford. Perhaps he would know something about the Scholarship.

Jonathan was restless, he couldn't stay cooped up in his Rooms, nice as they were. As he went down the stairs, he saw a strange sight on the far side of the quadrangle. Jason was dressed in a set of camouflage clothes and was marching along with what looked like a huge pair of compasses in one hand. He was twisting his hand to and fro, causing the ferrules at the end of the legs to clack onto the paving stones. It was an exercise in precision that Jonathan had never seen before. He strolled over just as Jason completed one side of the square. When he saw Jonathan, he snapped the compass legs together and placed the implement under his left arm, one hand holding the joined end pointing forward, and frighteningly parallel to the ground. He stood there, poised on the balls of his feet, leaning slightly forward. He barked, "Thirty paces exactly, SIR!" which echoed around the quad and launched a small flock of pigeons.

He grinned broadly at Jonathan. "Once a guardsman, always a guardsman," he laughed.

Jonathan was intrigued, "Can I see the...," he paused, not sure what to call it.

"Pacestick, sir," said Jason, as he flipped it from under his arm. Jonathan examined it; it was a thing of beauty, mahogany and brass, spotlessly clean and brilliantly polished. He tried to make it flip the way Jason had, but it required far more manual dexterity than he had.

"Took me a year to master it, sir, then I started winning competitions. There's a whole school of experts at Pirbright, if you can believe it."

Jonathan wondered whether a tape measure might not be more efficient, but managed to keep the thought to himself. He walked with Jason to the Porter's Lodge where Jason provided a mug of tea. He discovered that Jason had been forced to retire at the age of forty-two.

"There were too many senior to me, sir, blocking any promotion. But I had a wonderful career, Company Sergeant Major at Sandhurst for three years – best job in the world. I saw a few Princes and Dukes pass through in my time."

Jonathan had no idea what that implied, but nodded wisely.

"Interested in the military, are you, sir?" asked Jason.

It took Jonathan by surprise; he had never thought about it much. There had been compulsory Cadet Force at Standish and he hadn't minded the mild form of discipline. Then he remembered about the shooting; they had only been allowed to fire the small bore 0.22 inch rifles, but he had been among the very best shots; he had enjoyed mastering the technical features of such a powerful weapon. In the end Jason persuaded him to come to the Drill Hall that night to meet some of the Special Group.

When they got to the Drill Hall that evening, the place was almost empty.

"It'll be much busier when the Term begins, sir," said Jason, disappearing into a storeroom. He returned with one of the strange looking jackets that Jason himself was wearing and persuaded Jonathan to put it on in place of his old school blazer.

He blew a whistle that echoed around the grim Hall and several men appeared as if by magic. They were wearing the same uniform as Jason and stood to attention in a small squad.

Jason barked, "**Stand Easy**," and introduced them one by one.

"They're all from my Regiment, all retired for one reason or another. They like to keep close to the military life, sir, and keep their hand in."

Jason winked, for a reason that escaped Jonathan.

"We're practising unarmed combat tonight," he said in an aside.

Jason came to attention. "**Prepare for unarmed combat**," he roared, his voice booming around the exposed rafters.

Jonathan took a step backwards in surprise. He watched the men come to attention, turn in unison to their right and run to the side of the Hall. They seized a set of five coir floor mats and dragged them into the centre of the Hall. He was fascinated by the show of precision; it was like the workings of some fine mechanism, every movement calculated to bring an effect. The operation ended with two men standing at either end of each floor mat. One end of the mat nearest Jonathan and Jason was unoccupied. Jason laid his pacestick down with care and strode to the vacant spot.

"**Begin**," he roared.

A scene of such frenetic action commenced that Jonathan couldn't adequately follow it. Arms and legs moved with alarming speed, blows were countered almost before they began and one man after another landed with a dull thud on the mat. Jason had his man on the ground with his knee in the man's armpit. The man was hammering the mat with his free hand.

Jason got up with a grin.

"Here, have a go," he said, steering Jonathan to the end of the mat where Jason's opponent was now standing in the ready position.

"**Roman style**," ordered Jason.

Jonathan was about to protest when he noticed that the man had adopted a quite different position, half crouching, his hands reaching forward. It looked like the starting position used in Cornish wrestling, just like the old days in the village where he was unbeatable. Without a lot of thought, he stepped forward. As soon as his foot touched the mat, his opponent reached out with his right arm to grasp Jonathan's shirt, but Jonathan had seen it all before. By instinct he turned anti-clockwise, grasped the man's arm with both hands and turned his right hip into the man's stomach. The man had nowhere to go but down onto the mat.

Jonathan released him and looked at Jason, who shouted "**Easy**" at the man who was in the process of grabbing Jonathan's ankle.

Jason was grinning. "Just as Harry said, Mr. Hare, you have a natural talent. Did I hear correctly, sir, that your throw comes out of Cornish wrestling?"

"Well, I spent most of my junior days wrestling with the other boys; I won a few local contests."

Jason turned to Jonathan's opponent.

"Did you hear that, Roberts?" he said gruffly, "You were thrown by a Cornish champion!"

"Never seen that move before, sir," smiled Roberts. "Would the young gentleman like to demonstrate it?"

There was now a crowd around the mat.

The two of them faced each other and Jonathan ran through the throw in slow motion.

Roberts looked at Jason.

"Permission to try it on the gentleman, sir?" he asked with an innocent smile.

So it was that Jonathan found himself flat on his back looking up at a small crowd of cheering men. They helped him up.

"Better show him the breakfall, sir," said Roberts.

Jonathan learned to use his free arm to slap the ground as he fell, thereby lessening the effect of the throw. He also got the feeling that he had joined some sort of club. Jason's men had shown him respect and a rough sort of camaraderie.

He left the Hall with Jason and as they entered the College gate, Jason said, "You'll understand, sir, that the Special Group is unofficial. We're allowed to use the Hall, but you won't find us listed as part of the Officer Training Corps."

Jason was watching Jonathan's reaction and seemed satisfied by Jonathan's nod.

"Don't be surprised if you recognise one or two of the men around the College, will you, sir? I call on them from time to time to carry out certain security duties."

Jonathan went up to his rooms feeling more settled than he had for days.

TWELVE

Thicker than Thieves

THE ENQUIRIES THAT COLIN DAVIES SET IN motion about ex-Chief Inspector Forsyth caused a red flag to come up in the Serious Crimes Division of Scotland Yard. When Alistair Henderson was notified, he was intrigued, particularly because the flag had been placed by someone in the Commissioner's office. There had been some high level rumour about another debacle that the idiot Forsyth had created; the man was still an embarrassment even after retirement. There was always some truth in a rumour, Alistair thought, and this sudden interest from the Society had to be followed up. Good job he and Colin Davies were on speaking terms, otherwise the Society was strictly out of bounds, even to him. He wouldn't mind another trip to that Wine Bar.

Lady Hecate had become increasingly irritated that she had been unable to contact Roger de Quincy. In the past, she had been put through with dispatch, but recently she had been fobbed off with some junior officer, nice enough fellow by the name of Davies she recalled, but he had been uncooperative. He had said something about being sure that Sir Roger would call as soon as he returned to duty. The man simply would not tell her where Roger was; she understood that Roger might be engaged in some affair of state, but she couldn't see why he was so out of contact that he couldn't at least acknowledge her call. She had spoken with other people who ought to have been in the know only to receive surprised answers as if they had no idea that Roger was unavailable. She was mulling over this annoying situation when Rutherford entered discreetly.

"There is a telephone call from the Palace, ma'am," he murmured.

Lady Hecate knew immediately who it would be – the Chief Messenger as she called him, sometimes to his face.

Colin arrived at the Wine Bar, pushing his way through the men wearing well padded suits and fancy shirts, some still with bands[34] around their necks. The noise was enough to drown out any conversation near the bar.

Alistair nodded to a corner seat near the only window. They fenced for a while before Alistair decided to dive in.

"Look, Colin, take it from me, I'm not going to poke my nose into Society business, but I have to know why you're asking about old Reggie Forsyth."

Colin tried hard to conceal his surprise, but it didn't fool Alistair, who added, "I'm asking because we have an ongoing interest."

"Oh, it's just a loose end, really," Colin tried, but Alistair would have none of it.

"You boys at the Society don't ask for official traces without a purpose, Colin," he said, jabbing his finger on the table to make the point.

Colin chewed his lip. He valued his relationship with the superintendent, and had an increasing sense that getting back into the regular force might become necessary if Sir Roger didn't recover.

He took a breath and said, "Reggie's got himself a job at Oxford University and something happened there that I need to know about, something to do with an attempt to discredit the Hare lad and ruin his chance at a Scholarship."

Alistair sat back and looked at Colin carefully. "And why would you be interested in that?" he asked.

---

34   A band is the white tie with two short tails that has been worn for centuries by barristers.

Colin smiled, "We have a top security job that requires his expertise, but he's being difficult; he thinks someone in authority tried to sabotage his scholarship chances."

Alistair had risen to his present rank thanks in part to a gift that, as far as he could tell, was a form of Celtic 'second sight'. Time and again he would get this tingling of the nerves that told him that something of major importance was presaged. He had been mystified by the chill whenever Hare's name had cropped up in the Commissioner's presence. But now the young man had raised a spectre a little too close to home. And Alistair was getting these muted vibrations.

The telephone conversation with the Chief Messenger was couched in the most cordial of terms, but Lady Hecate was left in no doubt that she was to carry out yet another mission of the utmost delicacy. When she heard the details she was, for once, lost for words. She was being asked to report on the situation presently causing Sir Roger de Quincy to be hors de combat, as the Chief Messenger had put it. He had seemed more than a little embarrassed when he explained that a special car would arrive at Eaton Square for her and that she must present personal identification when she got to the destination. He knew she would understand that the location was secret, even to her.

She put down the telephone with pleasure at receiving another exciting challenge mixed with consternation that it had struck so close to her own interests. And, if she had read the Chief Messenger correctly, Roger was presently located somewhere that was kept very close to the Society's chest. So Roger was either ill or had committed some serious offence. Surely not, she thought. In either case, it didn't help her solve her son's problem. She discovered, much to her surprise, that she needed to talk to someone.

Alistair hadn't felt so alive for weeks; the sense of an imminent revelation stimulated him to ask Colin pointblank, "Is this safe in a gambling club, Colin?"

This rocked Colin back on his heels. But what could he say? Unless he could get young Hare to tackle the safe he was likely to fail at the most important case in his career.

"Well, yes, but there are aspects that I can't talk about; I hope you'll understand?"

"Yes," said Alistair, "but where does Reggie fit in?"

"Hare seems to feel that my boss, and yours for that matter, turned against him and did something to jeopardise his chances at the Scholarship. Unless I can get young Hare over his resistance, there will be hell to pay. Perhaps Reggie can find out the truth."

Colin's face certainly reflected his concern, Alistair thought, and now he himself had a problem. He couldn't let Colin know too much, and had to guard against any premature escapade. He was convinced now that someone very high in society had left a marker in this club. He decided to try it on with Colin.

"So you need to get Hare to retrieve someone's marker?"

Colin's body language told him all he needed to know.

"See, I understand your problem, Colin, but listen to mine. We think the wrong people have got into that club and we need evidence to shut them down."

There was a tense moment.

Colin brightened. "Perhaps we can kill two birds with one stone?"

Alistair thought, not for the first time, that Colin Davies was nobody's fool; he had neatly moved the conversation away from the marker and its owner.

"So where does Reggie come in?" he asked Colin.

"Oh, very indirectly; if I can get the real gen on the lad's ridiculous idea about sabotaging his Scholarship, perhaps I can persuade him to cooperate."

Alistair could see no harm in that, so he passed over a contact number. "Reggie'll know it's official business; that number is the maroon[35]."

"And, Colin, get him up here to the Yard. Tell him it's Pandora's Box, he'll understand."

Colin knew better than to ask what the operational code meant.

Lady Hecate's husband had died some time ago. He had been quite high in Royal succession and was endowed with the appropriate rank and entitlements but was otherwise a quite forgettable gentleman whose hobby had been growing roses, at which he had succeeded to a remarkable degree. He had been much older than her, not unusual in those circles. She sometimes tried to remember what he looked like; they had lived that amicable but almost sexless life out of which they had managed to produce a son and a daughter, a duty discharged by her with no particular enjoyment.

She had had the occasional affair, entered into only when she had felt challenged by the man in question, challenged at a level so elevated that it was hard to decide what had motivated her, the sense of danger or the need to establish her dominance. If she had been asked to say why she had committed *adultery* – and there were only a handful of people brave enough to contemplate such a question – she would have been astonished at the charge.

She would have admitted to affection for her husband, in the same way that one could have affection for a pet, but she would not have felt that it had anything to do with sexual gratification. She had, of course, heard of women enamoured with the act itself, so tiresome and so fraught with unwanted consequences. She had naturally steered herself away from any conversation that might suggest that a woman could seek pleasure there.

---

35   A term used to describe special methods to contact some ex-policemen. A policeman's job doesn't end with retirement; he will carry with him case knowledge that may be needed urgently in the future.

Recently, however, a strange feeling of inadequacy had been troubling her. She had never felt unfulfilled in her life, but nowadays she found herself too often at a loose end. Not that there was any lessening of the demands on her time, but the pleasure she used to get from manipulating this situation or ending the career of that offensive newspaperman seemed to have faded.

When she looked in the mirror, she saw a woman of no particular beauty, rather a horsey sort of face if she was to be honest about it. What set her apart were a flawless complexion and a superior demeanour that left no room for discussion. Her figure was still slim and athletic, certainly not Rubenesque. If she wished for a comparison, and she once would have laughed at the thought, she might have chosen Goya's painting of the Duchess of Alba. Perhaps she could no longer claim the same pertness of breast, or smooth belly, but she was more comfortable with that painting than with any of Rubens' sensuous generosity. She caught herself in this flow of imagery with a start, followed by a wry smile. Just when had she begun to dwell on this subject?

Eventually she made a connection to William Galdraith, as she called him privately. Not a handsome man, nor particularly challenging, but what was the word, 'persuasive'? Perhaps, but was he persuasive enough to ignite these untoward thoughts?

The police team had returned from the Isles of Scilly, muttering to themselves about the missed opportunity. Some of them were referring to missing a summer vacation in a holiday paradise but that was allowed to go unremarked. The Commissioner was annoyed that the suspect had fled, tipped off possibly, surely not from their side? Impossible to pin the deposit of the bonds on the Bessemer people, the receipt made out to what he was sure would be a false identity.

Lady Hecate invited William Galdraith to dinner. He arrived expecting the usual formal affair, with people chosen brilliantly to complement each other. He was surprised to find that he was the only guest. It wasn't the first time, but he had thought those occasions to be merely consultations, enjoyable certainly, but undoubtedly of a business nature. She had rewarded him with almost clandestine favours, unsolicited directorships in companies in which he had expressed some interest, perhaps a year earlier.

He had never had the sense that her patronage had any ulterior motive, well, certainly not of the sort that would end in bed. He had enjoyed her company in a passive sort of way, and he had been amazed at the stories told in his club that centred on her ruthlessness. He had kept his own counsel, never responding to invitations to express his own views. That she went by the name Hecate in such circles seemed unnecessarily cruel to him, but he had recorded the fact nevertheless, thinking that there must be something to it.

She had gone to greater lengths than usual, he thought; there was something different about her, but he couldn't think what. They sat comfortably enjoying a cocktail, brought silently by Rutherford, that tall man-servant whose face seemed more aristocratic than many of her guests. Rutherford announced dinner and they went in to the dining room. When she slipped her arm through his, he thought it was just the usual practice, although it did seem a little odd when there were just the two of them. He noticed that she was wearing a perfume that he almost recognised.

The table was as short as he had ever seen it, but its length was still imposing. He was taken aback to see that the two places were set halfway down each side. The silver centrepieces, which he always admired, even if they did tend to obstruct the view, were now positioned at each end of the table. A floral arrangement of amazing delicacy, something Hilary would love, lay between them.

When the main course was about to be served, she nodded in Rutherford's direction.

"We have a treat for you, William," she said as Rutherford approached carrying a bottle hidden under a huge linen napkin. The butler seemed to be having trouble with his face, thought William, hoping she hadn't selected some rare wine that he would have to taste and make knowledgeable noises about.

Rutherford carefully drew the bottle from the napkin and presented it on his left arm, as if it was a treasure indeed. When William read the label he was astonished to see that it was his favourite beer, Wadworth's 'Six X', a brew only found in pubs in the Vale of the White Horse. He laughed with her; even Rutherford allowed himself a faint smile. She must have gone to great lengths to acquire the bottle. It was a gesture so human and generous that he was a little embarrassed.

She waited expectantly, one eyebrow raised.

He felt a surge of emotion that somewhat unnerved him. As he struggled for the right words, a vision came into his mind of that beautiful Vale glowing in the evening sun, with the scarp face leading up to the Ridgeway in the distance.

"What a wonderful surprise," he said. "One day I shall take you to see the source of this famous elixir!" He was surprised at himself, for 'elixir' was not a word he would normally use.

Reginald Forsyth, ex-Chief Inspector and presently Proctor of Abingdon College, sat in his office at home staring at the telephone. The 'maroon' light was flashing; there would be a message, he knew, and it would not be one he could ignore. He picked up the handset and listened. Sure enough he was needed at the Yard; Pandora's Box was open again. He smiled grimly at the rather overdone joke. The summons was unusually terse, he thought, as if he was already in trouble. Perhaps something he had done, or left undone had surfaced. He sighed and prepared himself for the meeting, unusually early the next morning.

When he got there, he was unnerved to find two colleagues who, as far as he knew, had nothing to do with Pandora's Box. He had never met Colin Davies, who was wearing his Inspector's uniform, and had rarely run into Superintendent Henderson, a high flyer who everyone knew headed Serious Crimes and certainly had the Commissioner's ear.

The superintendent started straight in with hardly any niceties.

"Something has come up that you can help us with, Reggie, a rumour that we have to quash quickly to protect the Force's reputation. The rumour has it that an attempt was made recently to sabotage a candidate's chance to win a Scholarship at one of the Colleges. You must have heard about it. The story suggests it involves some very senior members of the Force."

Reggie's astonishment overcame his years of self-control. So the summons was nothing to do with Pandora's Box. He was faced with one of the worst mistakes any policeman can make; he had somehow permitted discredit to fall upon the Yard.

If Alistair and Colin had suspected that Reggie was personally involved they might have been better prepared for what happened next. Reggie slumped forward, his head in his hands, saying "Oh God, Oh God!"

What had started as a simple information gathering exercise had suddenly taken on a new and alarming dimension. Alistair got up and closed the door to the small interview room.

Colin was shaken by Reggie's reaction. He hadn't taken Jonathan's statement seriously; surely it was ridiculous to think that anyone as senior as Sir Roger and the Commissioner would go to such lengths. But now he had to face the possibility that the de Quincy brothers had actually taken this action against the Hare lad. And Reggie had been involved, somehow.

Alistair let Reggie get hold of himself.

"Now, Reggie, no one's on a witch hunt here, but we have to know what happened so we can take the appropriate action."

Reggie blew his nose. "I've been used, sir, duped really," he said hoarsely. "I was told it was a matter of state security. I was given a document to put before the Committee that would disqualify a candidate who was a threat to the Nation. I knew the document was incomplete; there was no DPS number, but coming from such senior people what could I say? And the candidate was prepared, blew me out of the water, and knew about the missing DPS number all along. I'm in trouble with the

Master and Lord Galdraith; have to report next week. It'll probably be the end of this job." He sat back dejectedly.

Alistair and Colin exchanged glances, trying to hide their shock. But Reggie was so wrapped up in his own misery that he didn't notice.

Alistair was quick off the mark. "Well, thank you Reggie, you've told us exactly what we need to know. It'll help us prepare for any untoward questions."

Reggie looked up. "That's it?" he said. "What do I tell the Master? He and Lord Galdraith aren't fools, you know."

Alistair had an answer. "Tell them you've investigated and it was a case of mistaken identity. Proffer our apologies, sincere as you can make them. Say that the real culprit has been located and will be dealt with." He stood up, signalling that the interview was at an end.

The Bessemer Movement's Chief Executive was glad to be back at Tudor House. He had rationalized the episode in the Scillies, thankful that his precautions had paid off. Pity about the assets, he thought; had they been real it would have been the best opportunity to advance the cause that had come their way recently. Can't win 'em all, as his father used to say, just win the last one! So that pansy Sir Roger had seduced the Hare boy, and on his first assignment too. Perhaps, the Chief Executive thought, it might be as well; the Movement didn't need people as easily turned as that. Unless, and this thought came out of the blue, unless the boy had never been properly indoctrinated in the first place. They would have to learn something from this, improve the screening, perhaps. But the boys were so immature when first spotted and recruited. How could the Movement be sure that their education had succeeded? He would have to put something in place. Perhaps an examination of Hare's recruitment and progress would be a good idea. He made a note.

Colin and Alistair had got rid of Reggie and were now looking at each other in consternation. They were so inured to the hierarchical system of command that they couldn't at first comprehend how the Commissioner could be involved in something like this.

Alistair was first to speak. "If I know Sir Hubert, he will simply deny the whole thing; he'll say some idiot made a clerical error. I can't speak for your boss, Colin, but there must be something we don't know about behind all this. I doubt if we'll ever find out the real truth."

But Colin felt less sanguine. "I think there's something else going on, something personal, as if Hare has knowledge that threatens their careers. I thought it might be that Sir Roger was worried that Hare and Miss Victoria were getting too close, but it has to be something more than that."

Alistair didn't respond; but that didn't mean that certain thoughts previously lying dormant hadn't surfaced. He didn't like the picture that was emerging, particularly since it could be the beginning of a breach in his relationship with the Commissioner.

Alistair called the Head of Records, Clive Atkins, into his office and shut the door.

"Look, Clive, something has come up concerning the misuse of a DPS number. Can you tell me how this number gets assigned?"

Clive looked at the superintendent with narrowed eyes. Here was a tall story if ever he heard one. Who did he think he was fooling, some laverhead[36] from the pits[37]?

"Well, superintendent, it's not really a matter falling to Records, is it?"

Try that, he thought.

Alistair realised that he had underestimated Clive.

---

36   The word 'laverhead' is used in Welsh valleys to refer to an ignoramus, perhaps a corruption of 'laverbread'. An English equivalent is 'numbskull'; in the US 'doughhead'.

37   Welshmen are always sensitive about the traditional occupation of coal mining.

"Sorry, Clive," he said with a grin. "I have a problem with a document that appears to have been forged. But they forgot to put a DPS number on it. Why would they do that?"

But Clive wasn't going to fall into that trap either, certainly not from some bumped up copper with an Edinburgh degree.

"And what problem would that be?"

Alistair was in a corner. He couldn't hide behind security; Clive was probably cleared to a higher level than him. He'd have to come clean.

"Clive, what I'm going to say next is pretty much my guess at something that has been going on at the highest levels here. It might be dangerous to let anyone know what I'm thinking." He waited for Clive to nod.

"An SO-4[38] was prepared based on false information to threaten someone outside the Force. What strikes me as strange is that the document didn't have a DPS number on it."

Clive thought about his response.

"A civilian wouldn't know about that, would he, it's too technical."

"But the point is that the person did know, and was able to refute the threat when it was made."

Clive saw what was coming. He was furious.

"And you're thinking that someone in my section has passed on such information?"

Alistair put on his hardest face. Clive got up and left the room without saying another word. Out in the corridor he was smiling; his intern Charles Barnes was the culprit he was sure and the civilian would have been a St. Eligius graduate.

---

38   This was the administrative code for the Statement of Offences document.

THIRTEEN

Sleeping Partners

WHEN WILLIAM GALDRAITH WOKE THE NEXT MORNING he had no idea where he was. Memories came flooding back; after-dinner drinks in a small and rather too feminine room – what had Rutherford called it? The 'Lavender Room', that was it. He had been so slow to detect the charged atmosphere; well, he just wasn't prepared for it, was he? She was such an imposing person and so regal that sex had never entered into his thoughts. He shook his head in bewilderment; he was such a blind fool; they were widow and widower, so he should have been more alert to the fact that few such friendships exist without a sexual component. The hints had been there at dinner, the bottle of Wadworth's – such a thoughtful and unexpected gesture. And he really should have taken more notice of that tiny smile on Rutherford's face.

Once they had finished their liqueurs, she had taken the initiative in a way that avoided any awkwardness, reaching out for his hand and leading him up to her bedroom. She hadn't really needed to say anything. Their lovemaking had been reasonably successful he supposed, although he had been as pleased by the fact that she had held his hand all night.

He looked around, but of course she wasn't there; there was the propriety of the household to consider. He dressed and went downstairs. Rutherford appeared and without any hesitation shepherded him into the Morning Room, saying, "Madam has taken her breakfast, sir, and will expect you in the Lavender Room."

He indicated a sideboard equipped with the usual silver dishes and left William to his breakfast.

Sir Roger de Quincy had a visitor. She was introduced as a psychologist, after which it became obvious that she could expect resistance. She was used to this reaction and took her time to explain her methodology. The meeting did not go well. Sir Roger continued to look uncomfortable particularly when she explained that he would have to bring his troubles into the open, the theory being that healing could only begin when they had been articulated. Eventually it became clear that there was to be no cooperation. Those monitoring the conversation in another room raised their eyebrows. Sir Roger would be out of action for too long; a replacement would have to be found.

After breakfast, William went as nonchalantly as he could into the Lavender Room. He had never been invited there before last night, and realised that his lady friend considered it to be her sanctuary. She smiled at him and offered him coffee as though last night had never happened.

"William," she said, "I value our friendship."

He digested this cryptic remark and concluded that she wanted their relationship to go forward on that basis. He felt surprisingly comfortable with that notion.

There was a prolonged silence. Eventually she stood up.

"William, I have a problem and need some advice."

He nodded.

"My son is inclined to sow wild oats, I'm afraid, and this time he has gone too far. He has overstepped the mark in a gambling club, a new one, and is now heavily in debt. I have a friend who has helped in the past but I find that he is either unwilling or unable to help on this occasion."

William had listened quietly, wondering when the other shoe would drop. Gambling debts were not uncommon in these circles he knew, and arrangements were always worked out because it was not in any club's interest to get the wrong side of such powerful people. There had to be more; he would wait.

Lady Hecate had been scrutinizing William's face and had seen nothing more than politeness, certainly not the shock she might have expected. She drew comfort from his tactfulness.

"If that was all there was, William," she said, "I wouldn't burden you, but there are two additional concerns; the club appears to have no interest in an accommodation."

William knew she was keeping the real problem until the last. She took a breath.

"I am sometimes asked to take on delicate missions that might get mishandled if left to the usual authorities. A senior official in a position of considerable power has recently been taken ill and I have been asked to look into the man's continued suitability for the job."

She walked around the room, stopping every now and then to run her hand over an ornament or examine a picture. He understood that she was choosing her words carefully.

"My difficulty is that the official concerned is someone who has provided assistance to me in the past, assistance through which he has become privy to some rather unpleasant facts about my son."

He found her looking directly at him with an expression that managed to combine a plea for help with embarrassment, something he could hardly comprehend.

William did something that would have been unthinkable yesterday. He got up and put his arms around her. She stiffened for a moment, and then relaxed. He took her to a chair and made her sit down.

"I can see your difficulty, my dear," he said. "I understand that you love your son despite his behaviour. Tell me more about the official."

Lady Hecate found herself in another difficulty. How much could she say about Roger de Quincy? His position was entirely unofficial; he had no government department or enabling legislation and yet he wielded enormous power and influence. The Palace owed him some huge favours, although he would be the last person to use them to his credit. The family tradition of service to the Crown went back for centuries. And his brother was the Commissioner of the Metropolitan Police. All in all, she thought, one of the biggest challenges with which she had been faced.

"Actually, William, the man in question is not an official in the strict sense of that word. His position isn't secret or clandestine as some are. In fact, he is apparently the head of a perfectly legitimate organization that has all the trappings of a learned society. In reality, however, he watches over the interests of families that are under threat from the far left, socialists that have mounted a quite formidable initiative to undermine all that England stands for."

William wondered why she was being so coy; anyone with a seat in the Lords and who was a member of several prestigious clubs would know whom she was talking about. In fact, it was at the Athenaeum recently where someone had commented on Roger's ill temper. "Most unusual," the man had harrumphed. "Roger's the model of an English gentleman, don't you know? Never dreamed he'd be so damned unaccommodating."

William decided to honour her reticence. "And this man has acquired knowledge of your son's misdemeanours and is using it against you?"

Lady Hecate was horrified. "Oh, certainly not; he would never stoop so low." She stopped, frowning. "But he does have this knowledge and is now incapacitated, so I worry that others might get to know by default, as it were."

"Nevertheless," said William, "isn't it this concern, this personal aspect, which is causing you to doubt your objectivity?"

Lady Hecate looked up, startled, holding her hand to her neck in a manner that he had never observed before. There was relief and admiration in her eyes.

William smiled. "I can't think of anyone in England better equipped to carry out this mission. If the official is incapacitated, the sooner you make your determination the better. If he recovers, we will deal with that situation."

Lady Hecate heard the transition into a joint responsibility with a surge of pleasure that momentarily confused her. The last time anyone had done it that smoothly it had been her son and that had been a disgraceful shirking of his responsibility. William had simply taken on a share of her dilemma. It was such new territory for her that she sat for a moment with her eyes cast down. William took this in. "I'm not going to get involved with the current mission, my dear, it would be most improper. Your remit is personal, isn't it?"

Lady Hecate could only nod, for once unable to speak without a catch in her throat.

It was decided, then, she thought, she would deal with Roger first; her son's problem would have to wait.

Superintendent Alistair Henderson was looking with bemusement at the envelope and its contents. It had apparently arrived while the duty officer was distracted, and had not been logged in. The officer had carried it up personally with a strange look on his face. "First time I've seen that priority stamp, sir," he said. "I thought I should handle it personally."

It was clear to Alistair that it had come from the man who sometimes called himself 'Sir James', but the only thing it contained was a heavily embossed visiting card. The honorific caused Alistair astonishment and awe; he was looking at the card used by Lady Hecate in her normal social rounds. The telephone number had been underlined, the message obvious – he should telephone, and the sooner the better.

Lady Hecate had hardly made her decision to proceed with her investigation of Roger de Quincy when Rutherford entered.

"There is a telephone call from Scotland Yard, ma'am."

Lady Hecate took it for granted that Rutherford would have carefully vetted the call and would not have interrupted without sound reason. She listened as Alistair introduced himself and mentioned his lunch with 'Sir James'. Lady Hecate was gratified but not surprised at the speed with which the superintendent had been called into action. She invited him to visit her as soon as possible. "You will please take a taxicab," she directed. Alistair didn't need to be told anything more about the importance of propriety in Eaton Square.

Alistair decided that his remit from Sir Hubert gave him the necessary authority to follow up with someone who was clearly a close relative, if not the mother of the idiot playboy being threatened by the Club mentioned by Sir James. He would play it safe, though, so he prepared a memorandum for the Commissioner outlining his progress so far. He made a special copy for a file that he carried with him in the handsome leather briefcase that his parents had bestowed upon him so many years ago.

He was greeted at the Eaton Square address by a man-servant with an aristocratic demeanour and conveyed into a reception room. Lady Hecate introduced him to Lord Galdraith with a charming smile. "I have no secrets from his Lordship, you will understand," she said.

The conversational niceties over, Lady Hecate looked appraisingly at Alistair. "So you are the Head of this new Serious Crimes Division. You have achieved remarkable results already, I hear. And in such a short time; I understand that such major successes usually take a year or two to bring to fruition."

Her eyebrows were raised, indicating that he was supposed to respond.

The doubts about the summer's successes that had been roaming his subconscious suddenly rushed to the fore. The best he could manage was, "Thank you, ma'am, I was fortunate to inherit some well-planned operations."

Lady Hecate's success as a mediator was due in large part to her intuition. Had one asked her about 'body language' she might not have responded, thinking the term rather vulgar. Nevertheless, she noted some unusual discomfort in the superintendent and decided to follow her instincts.

"And how do you find working so closely with the Commissioner?" she asked conversationally.

Alistair relaxed a little. "He's easy to underestimate, ma'am; he has an encyclopaedic memory and makes decisions that the rest of us can only wonder at."

Lady Hecate thought that was almost as nice a turn of phrase as she would use herself. It did not signal complete admiration. She thought she might as well continue this line and see where it went.

"He has the advantage of many highly placed contacts, does he not?"

"Indeed yes, ma'am, but he never refers to them in front of his staff."

If Alistair thought that was a safe answer, he was wrong.

"What, not even his brother?" Lady Hecate's thrust was as unexpected as it was surgical, and caught Alistair very much off guard.

Alistair's change of position and hesitation confirmed that there was something going on in that field. It would be to her advantage to probe this further, she thought, but not now.

"Sir James spoke highly of you, superintendent," she said, switching on that charm for which she was famous. It was his cue to offer his services.

"Thank you ma'am, I hope I can meet those expectations. However, there are some complications that I must alert you to. We believe that the Club in question, while apparently under the management of a perfectly legal limited company, is a front for an American operation seeking to break into the market here."

It wasn't necessary for him to spell out the strategic importance.

William Galdraith interjected. "It sounds to me like an opportunity to kill two birds with one stone."

Alistair smiled to himself hearing an echo of Colin Davies' remark. The problem was that to open the safe required the services of Jonathan Hare who was understandably wary of risking his Scholarship. And if he had been attacked by the Commissioner and his brother the young man would be justified in avoiding such dangerous territory.

"There is another problem, I'm afraid. The Club will have placed the marker in question in a safe that only one person in England can open. And, for reasons that I can't divulge, we have been unable to persuade him to take on the task. So, even if we were able to enter the Club with a search warrant, we would need to overcome our man's resistance."

Lady Hecate's instincts told her that she had learned something of more immediate importance than digging her precious son out of another of his messes, so she ended the meeting quickly, offering her assistance in any aspect of the case.

Alistair went back to Scotland Yard keenly aware that the Lady had outdone him in the field of interrogation. His training and expertise had been in the breaking down of a suspect's resistance by the delivery of the right question at exactly the right time. He smiled ruefully, thinking that the term 'iron fist in a velvet glove' would be more than appropriate as a description of the Lady. And why on earth had she made that connection between the Commissioner and Sir Roger. He shook his head. He must guard against allowing the knowledge garnered from that idiot Reggie to shape his thinking.

Lady Hecate and William Galdraith sat for a while in silence.

"What did you make of that?" she asked, eventually.

"The superintendent is no match for you, my dear," he said. "I think he has some information that is of deep concern to him personally. When you posed the question about Roger de Quincy he was flummoxed. It's interesting that a high flyer like that should be caught off guard. So whatever he knows, it has affected his relationship with the Commissioner."

Lady Hecate looked at William with admiration. She had become accustomed to his quiet astuteness in business matters, but hadn't previously witnessed such insight into human behaviour. But, she thought, he must have developed that skill, otherwise he would not have been so successful in running his industrial empire.

"So something has happened to Roger to put him out of action, something serious enough to warrant an enquiry from the Palace, and there is something going on that involves his brother. Can we assume anything more than that?" she asked.

"It's always dangerous to assume, but it might provide some leverage when you visit Roger," he replied.

Lady Hecate nodded; he had put things into perspective and reminded her that her priority was to determine Roger's present condition.

Fourteen

Lady Hecate's Mission

L ADY HECATE WAS DRIVEN TO A COUNTRY house in the back of a huge car with the windows blacked-out. The elaborate security precautions annoyed her; the officials at the gatehouse had not shown any respect and simply demanded the documents specified by the Chief Messenger. It was only then that a rather grudging 'ma'am' entered the conversation. She sighed, thinking that while such protective facilities were unavoidable in any modern democracy, she had not expected such a cavalier reception.

She was escorted to Roger's bedside and shooed away the doctor and then the psychologist, who was nearly reduced to tears.

"Roger, wake up immediately!" she commanded, for she sensed that he was faking sleep. He grunted and opened one eye.

"Hello, Lavinia," he said acidly, "I thought they'd send you; just your cup of tea, this, bring back the lost sheep, what?"

Roger's use of her much hated first name was rather too familiar and an indication of scarcely disguised hostility. She decided on a counter-attack.

"Don't be absurd, and pay attention. You have nearly killed yourself, for no reason that I can discover. Your record is impeccable; in fact there are favours owed to you by the Palace that you have never had to draw upon. What you are to tell me is why this situation has occurred. If you don't convince me, Roger, well, you must know what will follow."

140

She had said this brusquely, but Roger had heard the undertone of compassion. He shifted uncomfortably. "Working too hard, I think."

She waited, but he refused to offer any further information.

"The psychologist's reports suggest that you have been uncooperative, Roger. Hardly the best way to get a clean bill of health, is it? And look at you, wrists tied to the bed, how undignified. I tried to get them to release you for our talk, but they were adamant. You have exceeded some threshold, Roger. I don't pretend to understand the jargon, but you must realise that time is passing. Someone must take over the Society if you don't get out of here soon."

She waited again, but he lay quietly, strumming his fingers on the bedspread, a sure indication of his wish to be rid of her. He had never been anything but politely correct in their previous meetings. He had saved her son from several uncomfortable situations to her knowledge, and his efforts on behalf of the Establishment were legendary. Her instincts told her to get up and leave but she simply couldn't.

She decided on a new tactic.

"So what have you and Hubert been up to? Something dark and sinister, I hear?"

The effect on Roger was astonishing. His body slowly stiffened until he was rigid, only the wrist constraints keeping him in place. His eyes rolled back in his head.

The doctor rushed in, saying, "You must leave us now, ma'am. Sir Roger will need to be sedated. He will be unable to have visitors for a while."

On the way back to Eaton Square, Lady Hecate was saddened by Roger's condition. But, she thought, my instincts were correct. Roger and Hubert had indeed involved themselves in something that was weighing far too heavily on Roger's conscience.

Hilary Magnette had discovered what the family crest on Jonathan's letter meant. She sat there, stunned. Of course it could simply mean that he had a friend in the family, female friend by the handwriting. She thought about him with that suit and that air of self-assurance that had caused Jason to acknowledge his status in the officer class. She felt a sense of inferiority, aware that her father's title was in recognition of service, and was not hereditary, so she was a commoner. And she could boast of no published family history, of no estate described in the Domesday Book, like the de Quincys. Her decision to toy with him in his rooms had been such a mistake; she had assumed he was just another brilliant technician; it was really embarrassing to think about it now. But a mystery man, she thought, worth investigating.

Roger was raised from his fitful sleep to be given his medicine. He knew he had been dreaming and tried to recapture the images. Something about his father, he was sure, stern and demanding, a familiar refrain in the background, as though court trumpeters were announcing an imminent audience. Then a procession entered through a doorway, all of them men, some with strange beards and whiskers, carrying flags proudly. They were looking over their shoulders at a younger man bringing up the rear, and after him – no one. Or was there? There was a shadow in the doorway, and perhaps another flag bearer coming. Try as he might, Roger could not bring the flag bearer into the open.

He lay there sweating, for the significance of the dream was suddenly clear; he had let down his family, he had produced no heir and the Baronetcy, so jealously guarded over all the centuries, would end with him. What a disgrace, he thought; so much loyal service all brought to nought.

When Lady Hecate arrived back at Eaton Square, she was disappointed to find a note from William to say that he had had to attend to some business and that he would telephone later.

She mulled over what she had decided to call Roger's obduracy, but the word she had used sat uncomfortably in her mind. She shrugged. Whatever term one employed, it was a tragic story, but she sensed, incomplete, as if there was something so traumatic that he couldn't bring it to the front of his mind. But it was all a bit academic, for her report would be simple. Roger would have to go.

William Galdraith had been asked by the Master to come to Oxford.

"Rather disturbing news; can't discuss it on the telephone."

When William got to the Master's Study, the Proctor was there, looking very nervous indeed, expecting the sack, William concluded.

The Proctor was standing, another bad sign.

The Master said, "I promised to get to the bottom of this scandalous affair that the Proctor initiated. Perhaps he should explain."

William thought the Master certainly knew how to distance himself from trouble.

The Proctor drew himself up and took a deep breath.

"I have a sincere apology to make. I hate to admit it but I have been suborned by people in whom I trusted."

William wondered how many times the Proctor had rehearsed this.

"A day or two before the interview, I received a telephone message to ring a number I knew well. There was a codeword that all senior policemen understand to mean top priority and highly sensitive. When I rang, I found myself speaking to Sir Roger de Quincy and, to my astonishment, the Commissioner, Sir Hubert."

William could hear the rehearsed phrases; he had a remedy for this sort of thing – too early to employ it, he thought.

"I'm ashamed now to say that I was flattered, can't think of a time I ever spoke to a Commissioner before."

He did indeed seem penitent, thought William.

"They explained that it was in the national interest that one of the Galdraith candidates be disqualified. They claimed to have discovered that this candidate had been, well, a key figure in a plot against the country. I was more or less commanded to place a document in his interview file, which you have seen. It came to me by a dispatch rider, in a sealed envelope – I have the envelope here if you wish to see it – so I was convinced that it was something of major importance. When

I opened the envelope and saw the Statement of Offences, I suppose I simply read the text, didn't look for the DPS number; no reason to, really, coming from such senior people. I was just about to set up a local police squad to capture the lad, when it finally occurred to me that the document was incomplete, but we had already put everything else in place for the interview. I confess that it would have been better to test its validity, but how could I? I thought that, if there was truth to the offences, it would come out in the interview."

William had been listening for the sub texts. He thought that the Proctor was an idiot, but his errors were excusable. The Proctor hadn't finished.

"What shook my composure during the interview was that Hare was so knowledgeable. The DPS number is, of course, critical, but it's far too technical a point for a young layman to deal with so authoritatively."

He looked shamefaced. "Rather shot me down in flames, I'm afraid. He must be a very astute young man, my Lord, in addition to his excellent examination results."

William heard some buttering-up, but discounted it.

The Proctor's voice took on another tone that was not lost on William. "I have followed up the embarrassing situation, my Lord, and it now appears that a serious mistake was made about the identity of the candidate. I am told that a clerical error led to the confusion and the Statement of Offences should not have named Mr. Hare."

William stared at the Proctor for quite some time. It was clear that damage control was in full force. What the Proctor had said was only too obviously a cover-up. He hid his anger.

"That it?" he demanded.

"Yes, sir, unless you have any questions."

William thought that, all in all, the real blame lay elsewhere. He decided on a form of punishment.

"Wait outside, please, Proctor, we will call you back if we need you." Let him stew for a while he thought, clumsy idiot.

The Master and William sat for a while, thinking the matter through.

William finally decided. "We were made to look foolish, I shall pursue it. Would you leave it with me? I shall talk to Hare myself; we owe him that. I can't help feeling that there is more to this than meets the eye, though. People at that level don't go to such lengths without a reason. What do you think?"

The Master had earned his position through a massive intelligence coupled to the guile necessary to navigate College politics.

He stared out of the window for a while, wondering whether there was anything to gain from his next point. He decided to launch it anyway.

"Did you notice the absence of dates? And the mention of the warehouse on the Thames? Wasn't there a hugely successful raid on a warehouse that resulted in the capture of that terrible Grey Gang? Any connection, do you think?"

William stored it away, thinking that his choice of Master hadn't been so bad after all.

But mention of the police action brought to mind the meeting with the superintendent. Could it be that Scotland Yard had uncovered the plot? It would certainly explain the officer's poorly concealed reaction. He remembered how his lady friend had slid in the question like a stiletto; what skill, one could hardly blame the superintendent; poor man would be having kittens, giving the game away like that.

But look at it this way, he thought, there was simply too much detail in that document to be shuffled off as a case of mistaken identity. Perhaps the only one who really knew was the Hare lad himself. William made a decision. He would have to talk to his Scholar; and who would be better to help him than his Lady friend?

William telephoned Lady Hecate and invited her to come to Oxford, but she demurred.

"Bit too soon for that, William," she said. He grinned, and suggested the 'Bear Hotel' in Wantage, which was the most historic town in the Vale of the White Horse, and the birthplace of King Alfred.

It's a pity that this King, born in the year of our Lord 849, is remembered for some trivial story about burnt cakes, for he is considered by many to be one of the greatest of all Englishmen, a Saxon King who travelled twice to Rome and who brought peace and sound government to his people.

Wantage is a market town, tracing its charter to the early thirteenth century, although most of its heritage buildings are from the seventeenth or eighteenth century. It has a statue of King Alfred in the market place and is surrounded by countryside replete with racing stables. The Ridgeway runs only a couple of miles to the south, although it takes sound wind to walk up the scarp face. The Uffington White Horse is less than five miles to the west.

As far as William was concerned, Wantage had this added attraction; it was in Wadworth country, home of the famous Six X beer.

When they met, they both felt a certain shyness, ridiculous really at their age. She had insisted they take separate rooms, although she had granted him visiting privileges.

It was still early enough to take the car and head west along the tiny sunken road until they saw the track leading to the White Horse itself. She had never been there, like so many English people who have never fully discovered their homeland. The wind was blowing, as it almost always does, but it was bracing and the view breathtaking. They walked along the Ridgeway, sensing old vibrations left behind over the thousands of years it had been in use. Both of them had things on their minds, each wondering whether it was appropriate to talk about them.

Lady Antonia had decided to return to Frodsham. When she arrived, Thomas was at the door.

"Lady Antonia, I am afraid that I have some bad news to impart."

Thomas was not often this formal, but she seemed not to recognise it.

He continued, "Sir Roger has been taken away and admitted into a secure establishment." She looked blank.

"Inspector Davies would like you to telephone him; it is rather urgent, madam."

She almost pushed him out of the way, but she did not go to the telephone. He was as shocked as servants in his position allow themselves to be. But his allegiance was not to her, it was Sir Roger who had signed him on and who paid his wages. He made a decision and rang Inspector Davies.

"Lady Antonia has arrived, sir," he intoned. "She appears not to have understood the situation at all."

Either that or she doesn't care, he thought.

Lady Hecate and William had reached a spot where the edge of the Ridgeway had a small bank. They sat down on the travel rug from his car.

"This is very nice, William," she said. He understood that her comment applied to far more than the view; he felt the same contentment. He put his arm round her shoulders.

After a while, she asked him if he knew what she did with her time.

He had a pretty shrewd idea. "Sort out nasty problems for very important people?"

She looked at him sharply, thinking that he was a bit too accurate for her comfort.

"Yes, well, it wouldn't do for anyone to think that you know too much!"

He understood.

She thought for a while. "I have completed the interview and I will have to end the man's career. I once respected him; he comes from generations of loyalty to the Royals in matters that are never talked about. When I make my report it will probably result in his death. The man's in a terrible state, William. I've known him for years; he's helped me out so often, a real friend to the family."

William had heard the rumours of her son's behaviour, described as 'peccadilloes' by the higher echelon, but which would be criminal offences if anyone else committed them.

"We were right about the superintendent's sensitivity, William. Roger and Hubert have resorted to, well, some sort of behaviour so contrary to all that Roger stands for that he has had some form of attack. I will have no choice; I should have reported it already, but I needed more time."

And a shoulder to lean on, too, she thought, surprising herself.

William sensed her difficulty and drew her closer.

"While you were interviewing Roger, my dear, I was called to my College to hear a confession that may shed some light on this situation."

He paused, unaware that her sensors were buzzing.

"Roger and Hubert set out to destroy the reputation of one of my candidates, a young man called Hare. They used a fake document that only they could have produced; fooled me and my committee members, I can tell you. Thing is, young Hare seemed to have prior knowledge; saw right through the plan, shot down my Proctor, made him look like a fool. I've no idea why they did it; claimed it was a matter of national importance or something. The Master thinks it's somehow connected to that Grey Gang affair."

To say that Lady Hecate was stimulated would be an understatement. So there *had* been a situation that had caused the two brothers to take such an immoral action that it had been the undoing of Roger.

Her mind, already made up about Roger, turned to Hubert, and then moved away. He would be fireproof by now – no conscience, no trauma, he'd deny everything. Besides he was too much in the public eye, damn man made an art form of it; removing him would cost more than it was worth. But she would do something!

She moved on to this fellow Hare. How on earth could he have been prepared to face down a selection committee probably set up to intimidate candidates, using every trick in the book if she knew William. She decided.

"Would you let me talk to this young man, Hare isn't it?"

William was surprised, but sensed that another element had entered into the situation.

148

Fifteen

Special Relationships

BRITAIN AND AMERICA FORMED A 'SPECIAL RELATIONSHIP' during World War II; as a result the US Office of Strategic Security had a presence in London. By 1947 the OSS had become the Central Intelligence Agency with an entree into the British Intelligence community. CIA officers were present for at least some of the agenda items at meetings of the central British Intelligence Committee, even if British officials strenuously denied it.

Some in the community considered that it was more than useful to both parties to have an unofficial way of passing information at senior levels; on occasions this included US domestic concerns.

It was during a break for what the British called coffee that a CIA officer approached the member from MI5 to ask him to relay a message to the appropriate British official. A US citizen of interest called Joe Blanco was known to be in London, and if he could be apprehended it would be favourably received. This found its way through the murkier corridors of Whitehall until it reached 'Sir James'. A telephone call to Alistair informed Sir James that the Commissioner had been briefed. He told Alistair that he could expect to receive further details.

Alistair waited for the envelope sealed with a priority stamp used only by 'Sir James'. When he opened it, the contents gave him at most two days to set up an operation to apprehend this Joe person. As he read the material he began to see a pattern. Joe was a senior operator for an

American organised crime syndicate with particular interests in gambling and extortion. The connection with the Mayfair club couldn't be a coincidence. So now there was ample justification to act. But wait, he told himself. He couldn't go to a magistrate to obtain a warrant; this evidence was classified and in any case quite circumstantial. No, he'd have to rely on his existing plan and hope to catch Joe in the club. He picked up the telephone. It was time to start the ball rolling.

Jonathan's telephone rang; it was Jason.

"I have Superintendent Henderson for you, Mr. Hare," he announced.

"I hope this isn't too short notice, Mr. Hare," said Alistair in his smoothest and most confident voice. "I would like you to come for that briefing. The team will meet you at the Lodge at noon tomorrow. We are quite a lot nearer now to closing the noose on the person who is threatening you." Jonathan was reassured by the superintendent's manner; besides, if they finished early perhaps he could drop in and see Victoria.

The next day Jason telephoned him to say that two people were waiting for him at the lodge. He went down and was taken aback to find Charmaine there with a man he only half recognised. Charmaine had a hard look on her face; it was the man who spoke.

"Mr. Hare, my name is Sergeant Dobson. I was the barman in the 'King's Head' when you brought down Ronnie. You know Charmaine, of course." There was perhaps more emphasis on the word 'know' than was proper.

Charmaine put out her hand and said with no trace of the French accent she had employed when they last met, "Mr. Hare, I'm glad to be part of the superintendent's team."

She was all business, as if the kiss she had given him on the dance floor had never happened.

They left the Lodge and walked down to the station.

Jason watched as the donkey jacket strolled out of the book store and followed at a discreet distance; if donkey jacket tried anything he'd find out about unarmed combat in a hurry.

The team arrived at the station without incident and took the train to Paddington. Jonathan noticed that they selected a compartment with reservation stickers on the window, a practice that was unusual on a semi-fast train.

Charmaine sat in a corner and refused to look at Jonathan; it was left to Sergeant Dobson to carry the conversation.

"Tell me, Mr. Hare," he asked with genuine interest, "where did you learn that move you put on old Ronnie?"

They chatted about life in Cornwall and the almost religious fervour that surrounded Cornish wrestling. Jonathan had found an illustrated book about the 1936 Olympics in the Standish College library and worked out that the Cornish approach was pretty close to the Greco-Roman style.

"Of course," said Jonathan, "there was trade for tin between the Phoenicians and the Cornish from the earliest times; perhaps that's how it got there."

The sergeant talked about some of the throws and take downs used in police training, which interested Jonathan. He remembered Freddy in the warehouse boasting about knowing judo; he'd said something about getting his black belt soon. He'd have to practise it in prison.

The time passed quickly; they arrived in the great arched terminus of Paddington with Charmaine having contributed nothing to the discussion.

Arthur Salmon received the news he'd been waiting for. The target was on the way by train to Paddington. Arthur had got his hands on one of the Gang's taxis after the raid and used it to get around town. Put a cap on your head, he thought, and no one would look twice. So he gave instructions to a team of four men to use the taxi to get into the great Terminus.

Jason telephoned Harry. "The superintendent's team picked up our man at noon."

Harry hopped on a tube from Tower Hill and arrived at Paddington in plenty of time for a butcher's[39] around the arrival area. He scouted a position between the platform for the Oxford arrival and where taxis would pick up passengers. Paddington Station permitted special vehicles like taxis to enter the Terminus on a one way road that formed a taxi rank; a ramp rose from the platform allowing this traffic to drive out of the station. Paddington had another strange characteristic; arriving passengers for the major express trains would be dropped off at a special entrance off Eastbourne Terrace.

Charmaine spent the journey looking out of the window. She had seldom felt more uncomfortable and for a while couldn't understand why. Certainly being cooped up with the Hare lad was difficult; it was a constant reminder that she'd made a fool of herself when they danced. She shouldn't have lost control even for those couple of seconds; the memory of that moment continued to haunt her.

She hadn't known anything about him until that night in the 'King's Head' when he brought Ronnie Grey down with a flying hip throw. There had been something so physically attractive about the move that she had gushed a bit, and had to pretend to be flirting. She had caught Rita's eye, full of hostility, warning her off. It had only made Jonathan more interesting.

He'd said he didn't know how to dance, but he had responded to her teaching so well that she thought his claim was just an act. The worst part was that he seemed totally unaware of his physical attractiveness; or had that been an act too? She tried to get control of herself. She had a job to do, to protect the lad from any attempt by that Arthur Salmon. But behind her attempts to persuade herself was the suspicion that there was more to this operation than just minding him. The superintendent had something else in his hip pocket, she was sure of that.

---

39   Butcher's hook, cockney slang for 'look'.

The man in the donkey jacket had taken an empty compartment three behind the one occupied by Jonathan and the team. He was annoyed by the middle-aged couple who got on just as the train was leaving. They sat opposite and conversed in a country accent. He had some difficulty understanding them, not that he wanted to know what they were saying. It wasn't until the train was pulling into Paddington that the man spoke intelligible English.

"Bill Cousins, you'll be coming with us. Superintendent Henderson wants a word with you."

The woman was grinning and holding out her warrant card.

The train came to a stop in Paddington Station with its engine resting against the buffers, hissing steam. As the team walked to the ticket barrier Jonathan took a moment to admire the ubiquitous Hall class engine. While it couldn't compete with the Castles and Kings, it had no problem hauling the semi-fasts like the ones from Oxford to London.

They walked through the ticket barrier and turned right, heading away from the normal pick-up spot, which took Harry by surprise. Behind him he heard tyres squealing; he turned just in time to see a taxi racing up the ramp. "Someone must be in a hurry," he thought.

Sergeant Dobson had been told not to take a taxi from the internal rank, which was why he'd led the team towards the Eastbourne Terrace exit. Alistair had assumed that Arthur would try an abduction with a taxi from the Gang's own fleet; that would make it too easy. Alistair wanted to play Arthur for a while.

The unmarked police car located on the ramp off Eastbourne Terrace had a number plate readily recognisable by the informed, which included the Railway Police, sometimes called 'bluebottles' by the locals. It was their job to remove vehicles parked on the ramp. The team got in and were transported smoothly to Scotland Yard.

Jonathan was taken up to a small interview room where Superintendent Alistair Henderson was waiting for him. He greeted

Jonathan with a warm smile and firm handshake. Jonathan thought he could get used to such treatment.

"Mr. Hare, I'm glad to have met you at last. There's been a lot of talk about your part in the capture of the Grey Gang, but it's been kept under wraps. From what I hear, you looked after the young lady well."

Jonathan noticed that the young lady's name wasn't mentioned.

"And did I hear correctly that you were able to persuade one of them to spill the beans about the meeting?"

Jonathan thought he could see where this was going. He'd have to tread carefully otherwise they might find out about the bearer bond that he'd acquired.

"Yes, sir," he said. "I knew what Arthur had in that safe and when I told Sailor about it, it took him by surprise. He was so angry that he decided to get his own back on Arthur."

"And what did Arthur have in the safe?" said Alistair with the same wholesome smile.

Jonathan thought the superintendent might not know the answer so he'd try some misdirection.

"Some sort of bank notes that looked to be worth a thousand pounds each. About half a million I should think. Anyway that's what I told Sailor."

"And when did you learn that?"

"I was called in to open that safe earlier; Bert Coleman had forgotten the combination, and I couldn't help but see the notes when I got the door open."

"They weren't English banknotes were they?" The smile was still in place.

"No, they were foreign, a Bank from San something or other, I think it's in South America." There, he thought, that's a reasonable assumption and might keep the superintendent from finding out about his bond. And safeguard Count Paul too.

But the superintendent wasn't finished.

"Would that have been 'San Marino', by any chance?"

"Yes, it could have been," said Jonathan, frowning to add some doubt.

"I need you to be sure, Mr. Hare," said the superintendent, "it's an important piece of evidence if we're going to put Arthur away." He was smiling again. He pulled open a drawer and put a piece of paper on the desk. "Like this?" he said, pushing one of the bearer bonds forward.

"Yes, sir," said Jonathan, putting some surprise into his voice.

The superintendent pushed another piece of paper across the desk.

"Please sign this," he said; he wasn't smiling now.

Jonathan read a prepared statement, thinking that the superintendent's smile was like the Cheshire Cat's; it just vanished into thin air. Anyway, since there was nothing he could do now, he signed the statement where the superintendent indicated. And nothing had been said about his bond or Count Paul either.

The middle-aged couple took Bill Cousins to the Yard and handed him over to Sergeant Dobson. Charmaine had disappeared, hardly saying goodbye to the sergeant, who shook his head wondering what had upset her apple cart.

He sat Bill down behind a table with a telephone.

"Now Bill, we've got you for aiding a kidnapping, so don't play funny buggers with me. See, if you work with us we can find a way to forget your involvement. We know you weren't in the Gang – freelance weren't you? When did Arthur get in touch?"

Bill was shocked by the sergeant's view of his involvement. Arthur hadn't said anything about kidnapping, just 'keep an eye on the lad at Oxford' was all he'd asked for, so Bill wasn't about to go down for a rat like Arthur.

"About a week ago, Sergeant," he whined. "Arthur never said nothing about kidnapping."

"OK, Bill, perhaps we can work something out. What we want you to do is telephone Arthur and pass a couple of messages." He handed over a sheet of paper with the messages crafted by no less than Superintendent Henderson.

Harry had followed the team and seen them getting into the unmarked police car. He thought it was a bit clumsy; no other car would be allowed to park just there. And if he knew the number plate, others in the 'trade' would know it too. Anyone flying as close to the law as Harry would have to get hold of those numbers, just part of the cost of doing business.

The statement that Jonathan had signed was sent by dispatch rider to the duty magistrate; a warrant to enter the club premises to arrest Arthur Salmon was issued. It would arrive back within the hour.

Alistair settled down to apply his charm to Jonathan. He needed to extract more knowledge of the plot to discredit the lad at his Galdraith Interview. He could imagine how shocked the lad must have felt when Reggie presented that document; then he remembered the young man had been warned ahead of time.

"I understand that you were the successful candidate for the Galdraith Scholarship. Good show! But I hear that there was confusion concerning some document or other?"

Jonathan managed to keep his stone face in place. "My mother has a saying: 'All's well that end's well'."

Alistair realised that the young man had developed some resistance to his method of questioning. It had taken him longer to extract the facts about the bearer bonds than he'd expected. In both cases Alistair began to think that there was more to the issues than the lad had admitted. He would have to change tactics.

"The Proctor at your interview is an old colleague of mine; he's explained his side of the story to me. I'm not sure that he got it right though, Mr. Hare." The smile had reappeared.

Jonathan was aware that the superintendent was fishing. He decided to run a diversion.

"I'm glad that the interview came out well for me, sir. Now that I am the Galdraith Scholar, I need to keep my nose clean; Lord Galdraith expects that of me."

Alistair sat back, amazed at the sudden turn of events. What had the young man done now? Issue a warning not to push too hard? Surely not; but that was the size of it. He would have to produce a counter.

"Young man, I appreciate that Lord Galdraith wouldn't approve of anything that would bring discredit to the Scholarship. But I have to tell you that his Lordship would also recognise when the national interest is at stake." The smile had been switched off again.

It was Jonathan's turn to respond.

"I don't see how the award of a Scholarship could have anything to do with the national interest, sir."

Alistair realised that he had opened a door that he should have kept shut. It was time to reconsider his strategy. There was a remedy.

"You know, young man, I'm dying for a cup of tea. Why don't we pop down to the canteen?" The smile was back.

Jonathan hid his relief, agreeing with a nonchalant shrug.

In any service organization, the canteen or mess hall is an essential facility. Even MI5 and its sister agencies have them. Apart from their obvious usefulness, they provide a haven of sorts where the operatives can relax and relieve some of the daily tensions. One of the side effects, however, is that they accommodate a hotbed of gossip and speculation.

The superintendent was not a regular visitor to the canteen, preferring to take his tea in his office, so his arrival caused some stares and comments that were privy to the immediate company. The superintendent led the way, pushing his tray along and taking a large mug of tea. Jonathan followed his lead. They found a table in the corner of the room. On the far side of the room and hidden from Jonathan a group had taken a sudden interest in the new arrivals. Charmaine had found her way to that table; she was still upset over the meeting with Jonathan.

Alistair looked around the room. "Fine body of men and women," he muttered.

Jonathan thought it was a bit lukewarm, as though it was an expected sentiment. He decided to launch another diversion.

"Yes, sir, I know Inspector Davies quite well; he stood by me in some difficult circumstances."

Alistair put his cup down slowly. This confirmed that Colin had been in the dark about what Sir Roger had been planning. He hadn't doubted Colin's reactions to Reggie's story, although it had stretched his belief system at first. If Colin had been minding Jonathan and didn't know the overall plan, it must have been really under wraps from the start.

Charmaine's colleagues at the table had been on the Grey squad and several had been in Grey Central for the briefings. They had recognized that she was not her usual ebullient self. When they pressed her she muttered something about 'skeletons in my cupboard'. Eventually her body language caused one of the women to look over to Alistair's table.

"Who's the baby face, then?" she asked. Charmaine shrugged.

"Come on, Charmaine, he's not been here before yet he's giving you kittens."

Charmaine had been bottling up her annoyance, but couldn't contain it any longer.

"If you must know, he's the one that put Ronnie down in the 'King's Head'."

Her colleagues took a moment to digest this; they remembered that she had been ordered to 'give him the works' by the Commissioner. It had the potential for a juicy piece of gossip; several of them turned and looked.

"He deserves a medal," said one. "I heard he had a big part in the warehouse caper too, and got Sailor Wilson to spill the beans. If he hadn't we'd never have got the patch bosses, what a round-up that was."

"What's his name, then?" asked the woman, innocently.

"Jonathan Hare, if you must know," said Charmaine. She got up and walked determinedly out of the room. She didn't look at Jonathan.

There were several raised eyebrows at the table. Something must have gone wrong. And what was the young man doing with that fast-tracked superintendent?

Alistair had noticed the sudden interest in his presence and could hardly have missed Charmaine stalking out like that. She had carried out the pick-up duty but had seemed disenchanted with the whole operation. Did she know something about the Hare lad, something that he ought to find out? She must have said something at the table because several people had turned to look their way. He looked with alarm at his watch; the timetable was urging him on. These other issues would have to be deferred until the operation had succeeded. As he prepared to leave, a detective in his Division came across and said, "May I shake Mr. Hare's hand, sir? I'm honoured to meet such a brave young man."

Jonathan reddened as he shook the man's hand. Alistair mumbled something about having to rush and took Jonathan's elbow. They left the canteen at something of a trot.

Arthur Salmon hadn't heard from his man tailing Jonathan for some time. Then a telephone call came in saying that the target had been taken away in an unmarked police car, so the tail had gone to keep watch outside the Yard in case the target surfaced there. This seemed reasonable to Arthur; his taxi squad had reported the failure at Paddington.

"Never even looked our way," one of them had grumbled. Arthur knew enough about the Yard's geography to realise that one man keeping watch could be fooled. He sent the taxi squad to drive around the area.

Alistair led Jonathan back to his office, looking at his watch rather anxiously.

"Look, Mr. Hare," he said, with his brow furrowed. "It's getting late. Have you eaten?"

Jonathan admitted that he was getting hungry.

Alistair shuffled some papers around on his desk.

"There's a few questions remaining, then I'll take you for a curry. There's a fine place not far from here, 'Taj Mahal' they call it, not very original, but the food's good."

Expecting Jonathan to demur politely, he held up his hand.

"No, no, it's the least I can do, dragging you up here like this."

Jonathan hadn't given any thought to turning down a meal that he wouldn't have to prepare for himself, so the superintendent's protestations held the day.

Harry went back to his house. Something didn't sit right. He telephoned Colin Davies and was shocked to hear that Colin didn't know that Jonathan was at the Yard. Colin detected some unusual concern in Harry's voice and got out the Wolsley and drove across to Harry's house as quickly as he could. When he got there the front door was open and he heard raised voices. He hurried in and saw Harry trying to pacify a young woman.

"Oh, Colin, this is Charmaine Montpelier, she just got here. Something's up at the Yard. Charmaine, this is Inspector Colin Davies."

Charmaine had already recognised that he was a copper. Nicely set up, too, she thought distractedly.

"Which division, sir?" she asked.

Harry rushed in, "Colin's on a special assignment," he said quickly.

Charmaine looked at him and grinned. "You're not a black boy, are you sir?"

Colin had a ready answer. "Well, you won't find me at the Yard."

He thought her smile had transformed her. Perhaps she wasn't conventionally attractive, but she certainly knew how to present herself. But what was she doing here?

Harry interceded. "Look, Jonathan's at the Yard with Superintendent Henderson, the one that's in charge of Serious Crimes; he's got hold of him. We both think he's using him in some way, but we don't know how. Charmaine did the pick-up, but she didn't like it; apparently the super asked him to come for a briefing about Arthur Salmon."

Harry's expression indicated that he thought this was eyewash.

Charmaine said, "No one knows I'm here. I don't have anything that would stand up in court but, well, we've never seen the super down in the canteen; he thinks he's too good for it. So how come he brings Jonathan down there? I think he's trying to get a special relationship going with the lad; he wants something and he's using Jonathan."

Colin was in a quandary. It was clear to him that Alistair was trying to persuade Jonathan to open the safe, but he couldn't tell Charmaine that. He took a moment to think about the image of Alistair in the canteen; bit of a laugh really. Then it struck him. The real question was why Jonathan was in London. Colin recalled that he'd had to go down to Oxford to try his luck with the lad, but Alistair had somehow got the lad to come up to the Yard of all places.

Harry was watching Colin, thinking much the same thoughts. Jonathan was reasonably safe in Oxford, but now he was far too close to Arthur's place. Protection was called for.

"Look, I think we should get ourselves round to the Yard. We may be able to do some minding if it's needed."

Colin nodded. "We'll take my car; it'll get us into places out of bounds to mere mortals." He smiled, asking himself whether he was trying to impress Charmaine. Harry had certainly given him an old-fashioned look.

And he didn't hold back on the way to the Yard; there wasn't much point being a specially trained driver if you didn't put it into practice, was there?

Alistair sat Jonathan down in the interview room.

"Tell me why you got the wrong side of my Commissioner."

The question came so unexpectedly that Jonathan flinched. It told Alistair something new; the lad had given the first sign of not being in control of his emotions. And it made it clear that the young man felt scared of Sir Hubert. Yes, thought Alistair, I'd be scared if I'd been subject to wrath from that quarter.

Jonathan had got his stone face in place. "I think you'll have to ask the Commissioner that. I only met him a couple of times."

"And when was that?"

"Once in Sir Roger's office and once after the raid on the warehouse."

"Tell me about the meeting in Sir Roger's office."

Jonathan frowned. "Well, sir," he said, deciding to give Alistair a semblance of respect. "I think they were testing me. Then they told me they needed my services."

"And what services are they?"

"To open safes for powerful people."

Alistair digested this; it fitted with all he knew of Sir Roger's operations. But why was the Commissioner there? He may be Sir Roger's brother, but his presence had to have more significance than that. The brothers must have had another, longer range strategy in mind.

But that would have to wait. His was getting behind his timetable.

He got up. "Let's go and have that curry," he said.

They walked down a corridor, stopping at another interview room. The superintendent opened the door.

"Number Two," was all he said, holding the door open for rather longer than was necessary.

Jonathan caught a glimpse of a man in a donkey jacket. So they had rounded him up. He began to feel better.

When the door closed, Sergeant Dobson shoved the second telephone message in front of the donkey jacket.

"Make it now," he said with a smile.

SIXTEEN

Spice of Life

ALISTAIR LED JONATHAN OUT THROUGH A SERVICE door and across a yard into a side street. They walked at a fast pace down several turnings until they could see a better lit area ahead of them. Alistair took Jonathan's elbow and steered him along the road to the 'Taj Mahal'. He explained that Indian food had always been popular in England, the taste brought back by military and Colonial Office people. When the immigrants from that country started to arrive in greater numbers, Indian restaurants began popping up all over London.

The 'Taj Mahal' was more pleasing than most Indian restaurants in England at that time; the décor was splendidly ornate and the food was offered buffet style. Jonathan followed the superintendent and selected more or less the same. He found the food far spicier than he could manage, however, and sat there looking wounded. As soon as he took a mouthful of water, the pain increased dramatically, and he jumped up and hopped from foot to foot fanning his face. There was a burst of laughter and some applause and even Alistair permitted himself a chuckle, so neither of them noticed a thin-faced man get up and push through a curtain.

A young woman in a long and very beautiful silk gown hurried over, carrying a dish of a white milky substance. She smiled at Jonathan and said, "Quickly, take some of this!" and pushed a spoonful into his mouth. It immediately cooled him down.

"It is only yoghurt, you understand," she said in a lilting voice. "You are finding the curry too strong, I see. I will bring you something different."

She placed her hands together, fingers upright, as she bent slightly forward, smiled and seemed to melt away. She was extremely graceful. Almost immediately, she returned with a plate of food, saying, "This is what we eat ourselves; the food at the buffet is not for us, but you English are wanting it like that."

Jonathan said, "Thank you," and for reasons that he did not understand, mimicked the gesture that she had made with her hands. The young woman looked surprised for a moment, then smiled, and laughed. "If you come again, ask for me, Reka, and I will prepare for you something special."

Alistair tried to hide a smile; the lad was unaware that he had made a conquest. For such a composed and intelligent young man, he was hopelessly naïve.

Jonathan took a forkful and found that it was very mild, but far fresher and more aromatic. It created the same sensation that Charmaine's paté and cheese had, stimulating his entire mouth.

"This is good, sir," he exclaimed. "Would you like to try some?"

It was at that moment that the manager arrived and said something to Alistair, who stood up and said, "I'm sorry, you'll have to excuse me, an urgent telephone call, you know," and disappeared through a beaded curtain.

Almost immediately two large men appeared on either side of Jonathan. They were not policemen, he was sure of that.

"Get up quietly, son, and come with us."

Jonathan could see that he had no choice; he looked desperately around for Alistair, but he had disappeared.

Charmaine, like so many of her colleagues in France, liked to smoke Gauloises[40]. Her canteen friends pulled her leg unmercifully, with comments to do with frogs and smoking horse manure. She put up with this on all but her bad days, when she would sneak out through a small side door that few used. It opened into a small service area, where she could indulge herself free from the joshing.

When Colin skidded the car to a halt near the Yard, Charmaine got out with a sigh of relief. "Show off!" she thought, secretly pleased that he had put on such a show for her benefit.

"We'll have to split up to cover all the exits," she said.

Colin looked at his watch. "Meet here every fifteen minutes," he said, assuming command. Charmaine found that she didn't mind it a bit.

She had been well trained as an agent for the Securité and could move from cover to cover as invisibly as the best. She had already decided that if something was not right, the super might not want to be too obvious. She worked her way to the service area where she sometimes smoked her Gauloises. She waited in the shadows for a while. The door opened and the super and Jonathan came out and went quickly across the street. She tailed them to the 'Taj Mahal.' Assuming they'd be there for a while she hurried back to the car. Colin and Harry looked puzzled.

"Come on," she urged. "We need to get there avec urgence," she exclaimed, lapsing into her native tongue.

The two men moved Jonathan toward the door with professional ease. He could see no logic in the situation and no sense in resisting. He needed more information before making a move. When they got outside, one of them whistled and a taxi appeared from round the nearest corner. They got in without a word.

---

40   A pungent cigarette favoured by the French. At one time it was considered a patriotic duty to smoke a cigarette patronised by so many that fought in the War.

Colin had parked the Wolsley just down the street so they could observe the restaurant. The street was busy with traffic and Colin had placed the car across an entrance to a small park. Heaven help any young bobby trying to move him on. They watched the front door of the 'Taj Mahal'. After a while, two men of muscular build appeared with Jonathan between them. A taxi came from nowhere and Jonathan was bundled in.

Harry sat up. "Wait a minute," he said, "that taxi's not kosher; there should be a white licence plate below the number plate. I bet that's one of the Gang's taxis; they run them privately, never to hail[41]."

While they were digesting this, the taxi moved off. Colin put the Wolsley in gear, but before he could move another Wolsley slid into view.

"Blimey," said Harry, "that's a police car, see that number plate. And the back wheels are set a bit higher." He recalled that it had been Jonathan who pointed that out when they were on their way to help out Bert.

They watched as the unmarked police car let a small gap appear in the traffic before it pulled out. Colin recognised the surveillance technique; the aim was to follow, not intercede. He tuned his radio to the police dispatch channel and got into the stream of traffic, keeping a close eye on the other Wolsley.

In the taxi, both men had hold of one of Jonathan's wrists. Almost immediately one of the men slipped a blindfold over his head. He must be a professional, Jonathan thought, there had been no unseemly haste. The taxi was following a strange path with many sudden turns to left and right. Jonathan's palms were sweating. He had to keep calm, he thought, but that was easier said than done with a gorilla on either side, gripping him with fists of iron.

Taxi drivers in London are licensed by the Public Carriage Office and have to pass a gruelling test known as 'The Knowledge'. It takes most

---

41   A 'hail cab' was licensed to pick up passengers from the street on a 'hail' – a wave or a whistle.

applicants many attempts to pass the test, but it ensures that taxi drivers have an encyclopaedic knowledge of the road system anywhere within miles of Charing Cross. The police car immediately behind the taxi was taken by surprise when the taxi went completely round the Hyde Park Corner roundabout and slipped within an inch of a double-decker bus and off down Grosvenor Crescent.

In Colin's car, they heard an exasperated voice over the radio. "What d'you mean 'Lost him' you idiot?" This was followed by even stronger language rarely heard over the regulated airwaves.

Colin thought through the situation. The super had obviously set up something otherwise the other Wolsley wouldn't have been there to tail the taxi. If Harry was right, the taxi would be under Arthur's control. And Harry thought that Arthur might be hiding in the club. So where would they go? He cast his mind back to the Royal Person's file. What had that poncey idiot said about the club? Something about being near the Dorchester, that was it. He took firmer hold of the wheel and drove up Park Lane, turning at the front of the famous hotel shaped like a ship's bow. He parked in a Mews with double yellow lines on both sides, leaving barely enough room for any other vehicle.

"We need to scout the area, look for any property that'd pass for a Club, double front doors, lots of coming and going. On foot, back here every ten minutes."

The tone of command was back.

The taxi driver had noticed the tail earlier and was now sure that he'd shaken it off. He got on the radio to Arthur, who told him to bring the package to his place. By this time the taxi was driving round the Victoria station forecourt, ignoring frantic waves and whistles from people with suitcases. The driver turned the taxi and headed north for Mayfair.

Harry was adept at using street corners, a necessary art for a 'spiv'. What did they say? 'One round every corner, get you anything you want', that was it. You had to take your time looking round the corner; you didn't want a rozzer to bump into you. So Harry was pleased when he spotted a new 'R' type Bentley with its streamlined body easing up to the curb in front of a swish house. He watched for a minute or two and spotted several luxury models, including a beautiful Alvis, come to a stop in front of the house. He had often told his boys how to recognise money; it wasn't any good setting up anyone stony-broke was it? Anyone owning one of these cars would be a good mark. He strolled past the house and noted the double doors. He decided it must be the place, and trotted back to Colin's car.

The three of them got into 'box' watching positions. Harry was disappointed to be told to scout out the rear of the premises. It wasn't anything like as grand as the front, just the usual service area off a narrow lane still cobbled from the days when horses were stabled close to the grand houses. He leant against a doorpost and lit a cigarette.

The taxi carrying Jonathan and his captors took a route designed to confuse any tail that might have picked them up. Ignoring so many hails and whistles might just have caught the eye of a rozzer somewhere. It went up to Piccadilly Circus and circled the statue of Eros completely. Satisfied that he was still clean the driver slid through Soho and into Mayfair where he turned down the cobbled Mews lane. The driver didn't see Harry. It nosed into the service area. The two men took Jonathan's elbows and ushered him out of the cab. Harry slid away and found Colin.

"They've taken Jonathan in through the back door to the Club," he said, somewhat out of breath.

Colin sent Harry back to the cobbled lane. "Keep an eye open, Harry," he grinned. "You know where rabbits go when we put in the weasels!"

Seventeen

Connections

COLIN DECIDED THAT THEY WERE TOO SMALL a force to deal with the situation. There was nothing else for it, so he went back to the Wolsley and switched his radio to send. He demanded a direct link to Superintendent Henderson and got through surprisingly quickly.

"Sir, I believe we've located the young expert at the home of the suspect who is on the loose." He gave the address of the club. "We need a heavy squad here with a warrant."

Alistair gathered the heavy squad in the Operations Room. The Sterling Control team had already been brought in and briefed. When they saw the heavy squad with their sinister uniforms and equipment they stared like startled rabbits from behind their horn-rimmed spectacles.

Jonathan was led expertly through a door and up some stairs. By now he had no idea where he was. Eventually he was pushed downwards and his hands tied to the arms of the chair. The blindfold was removed and he found himself in a dimly lit room with a light shining in his eyes. Behind a desk in front of him sat a small, swarthy man. From the little that Jonathan could see, the man was wearing a white dinner jacket.

An image came to him of Harry laughing about how the Yanks loved wearing this outfit. "Call it a tuxedo, don't they!" he'd said. The conversation had turned to crime in the States and Harry had muttered something about crime families and their connections. When Jonathan had asked what he meant, Harry had looked astonished, and said, "You mean you don't know how them Mafia people operate?"

He'd sighed. "Look, they're big and powerful and work together when it suits them. Far as I know they haven't got a foothold here yet. But once you're part of the family they say you're connected. It means you can call on the power of the entire family and their associates. Bit like an octopus," Harry had said darkly.

"This him, then?" the small man asked.

Jonathan came to with a start. He was having difficulty breathing and the arms of his chair were slippery with sweat. But he remembered his schooldays and the usual bullying. He had learned never to show fear, otherwise it gets worse. Stand up to the bully and he may be a coward. Easier to say than do, he thought.

A voice came from out of the shadows, "Oh yeah, that's the rotten little bugger."

Jonathan couldn't see who was speaking, but he knew who it was. It was Arthur Salmon, the one who had kidnapped Jane and him.

The swarthy man was tapping the desk with a nasty looking thin-bladed knife. The blade shone in the desk light.

Jonathan was fighting his anxiety but he sensed that this was too theatrical, an act staged for effect. It reminded him of some magician's tricks; he might have to use some of his own.

"So," the man said, "this is Jonathan Hare, the famous safe-breaker and escape artist; he's a bit young, huh?"

Arthur spoke from the shadows again. "Don't be fooled, he can create more trouble than you'd believe; brought down Ronnie, and led the raid on the warehouse. Police contacts for sure."

Jonathan felt pole-axed, but managed to keep his stone face in place.

"So tell me, Johnny boy," the man at the desk said, "how come you know so much about our financing operation?"

Jonathan began to see where this might be going. Arthur's safe had all those Bearer Bonds, and perhaps they were used instead of cash; he had done some research and found out they were just as good, as he had discovered when Count Paul exchanged his Bond so readily. But he had better not let them know what he suspected.

"I'm sorry," he managed. "I'm stumped, I don't know anything about your business. I don't know who you are, but I recognise Mr. Salmon's voice. I *was* attacked by Ronnie and defended myself, but the police were waiting for him anyway. And I was at the warehouse; Mr. Salmon got Sailor Wilson to bring me there for his own reasons, and the police must have tailed Sailor's car."

He hoped that was good enough.

The small man let the light shine on the blade of the knife again, saying, "What he's talking about, what's 'stumped'?"

Arthur snorted, "Oh, it's a toff's term. He's saying he doesn't know what you mean, hah!"

Jonathan thought he'd better keep quiet. The small man was tapping the knife on the table in a faster tempo.

"But you are a safe expert and you do know what Arthur had in his safe."

Jonathan kept quiet.

"Perhaps you don't realise, Johnny boy, just what I can do to you. I don't like liars, do I Frankie?"

Frankie, one of the men in the car, laughed on cue. It sounded forced to Jonathan.

He thought there wasn't much point denying his expertise, so he said, "I have been able to open several Champions, yes, but that doesn't make me an expert. They're quite rare, too expensive and heavy for these times, and they're not made any more; the factory was bombed during the last war."

"Don't try and weasel your way out of this, Johnny boy. I know you know what was in there. Now, who else've you told?"

There was a silence. Jonathan decided that he'd better try some misdirection, and quickly.

"I wish you wouldn't call me 'Johnny boy', no one calls me that; my name is Jonathan, and I don't know what to call you, either."

The small man had started to raise himself, and the two huge men had moved a step closer to Jonathan. Then the small man subsided with a twisted smile, opining that Jonathan certainly had 'moxie'.

"You can call me 'Mr. White', for now," he said, clenching his teeth in what was intended as a pleasant smile.

This time Jonathan picked up the man's American accent clearly; it caused shivers to run up his spine. But he had to keep the man misdirected.

"Mr. White, may I ask you how long you've been in England?"

There was another silence. The man scratched his head.

"What's that got to do with anything?"

"Well, sir," said Jonathan, throwing in a gratuitous honour, "you'll understand that in England things are done differently than in America."

There was another silence that hung heavily in the air.

Arthur began to speak, but Mr. White silenced him with a flick of his hand.

"Go on, Jonathan."

Jonathan heard his name used properly for the first time.

"Well, sir, in England there are powerful people with connections who can look out for their friends, including me. And they don't like kidnapping."

There was a small buzz of interest in the room now.

"So, Jonathan, tell me who has that sort of juice."

Jonathan was stumped again, wondering what juice had to do with anything.

Mr. White laughed, "Juice, boy, juice, what would you say over here, influence maybe?"

Jonathan raised his eyebrows, hoping the American would work it out. He waited for a while, but decided he'd better speak.

"Haven't you recently had someone in your club with that sort of influence?"

Mr. White slapped his hand on the desk; it sounded like a gunshot.

"You mean that slimy bastard that left his marker?"

At that moment there was a loud banging somewhere below, and an amplified voice saying, "Open up, Police! We have a warrant!"

Jonathan was surprised at the reaction from the men in the room; they didn't appear to panic. Mr. White looked around and said something to the two big men that sounded like 'van moose', which he thought must be one of their codes. Mr. White nodded at Arthur and ran his finger across his throat. One of the men took something out of his pocket and swung at Arthur who went down in a heap.

"You're a smart fella, Jonathan, and I think you're connected too. Nice misdirection, you win the cigar!" and then he was gone, and the room was empty.

Jonathan heard a crash and footsteps running upstairs. Police entered the room to find a recumbent Arthur and Jonathan still tied to the chair. They shouted at him, "Where did they go?" so Jonathan nodded towards the door and said, "Down some stairs, I think."

Several policemen pounded down the stairs, leaving a couple behind to untie Jonathan. When he looked up, he was only mildly surprised to see the superintendent.

Harry had kept half an eye on the taxi, still parked in the service area. At the back of the house a door crashed open and three men rushed out. The taxi reversed into the lane and sped off. There wasn't anything that Harry could do. All he knew was that Jonathan wasn't one of the three.

Arthur was still lying on the ground. Alistair pointed at him and a policeman went over to attend to him.

Jonathan watched the superintendent come towards him and untie his hands.

"Are you alright?"

Jonathan didn't detect any genuine concern.

"Tell me what happened."

Jonathan shrugged. "I was picked up in the 'Taj Mahal'; a taxi came to the curb and I was pulled into the back seat. They grabbed my wrists and blindfolded me, and brought me here."

The superintendent smiled. "Come on, young man, don't play games, remember I know a lot about you from Inspector Davies. Give me everything."

Jonathan shrugged, thinking it would do him no harm, so he explained about Mr. White. When he described the American, the superintendent grinned. "I knew he was a cagey one, but his real name is Joe Blanco, married to the daughter of a Capo in Vegas. The family sent him over to get a foothold in the gambling scene. Arthur Salmon is their money-launderer, I'd bet on it."

Just then a sergeant came into the room, looking shamefaced.

"We lost them, sir, they had a taxi waiting. We got the number, but I doubt that'll help."

Alistair sent the sergeant to get the Sterling Control boys.

Harry had joined Colin and Charmaine in the Wolsley.

"Come with me," said Colin and they walked to the club. There was a moment's confusion before Colin showed his warrant card and they were allowed in.

They went upstairs where Jonathan was still rubbing his wrists. Alistair decided to put a brave face on it.

"Look, we lost the chance to grab the American but otherwise I think we can all be pleased at the outcome. All we have to do is open the safe and let the Sterling Control people have their way."

Colin frowned, "But what about the marker, sir?"

It was at this moment that a civilian in a pinstripe suit and horn-rimmed glasses entered.

"Superintendent, I thought you told us we'd find evidence here?"

Alistair nodded.

"Well, that's as may be, but no one can open the safe, it's an older model Champion."

"Ah," said Alistair, "We have the very man here!"

He looked at Jonathan, who shook his head, saying, "I can't open it without my equipment."

Alistair laughed. "Good job we brought it up from Oxford, then."

Jonathan looked with astonishment at his silver-sided case.

"Lord Galdraith gave Jason permission to retrieve it; he was intrigued by the situation. I told you he would be."

Jonathan felt betrayed; someone had invaded the privacy of his Rooms.

The safe was, as reported, a Champion, one of the simpler models with only fifty gradations on the dial. Jonathan thought it would be easy.

He opened the case and took out his special dual head stethoscope and monitored the tumblers. He twirled the dial, but the tumblers sounded stiff and unresponsive. He scratched his head, because the sound didn't fit with his knowledge of safes at all.

He looked down the side of the safe and spotted the model number; it had the 'X' prefix.

He recalled that the Mountbeck safe was also an experimental model, not documented in any of the manufacturer's literature that had survived the Blitz, and that it had had a peculiar extra security built into the functioning of the opening handle.

He applied pressure to the handle and found that it could be moved into the 'up' position and twirled the dial again. To his relief the tumblers started to make the sounds that they should. It took him just under an hour to detect the five dial positions.

He called out to Alistair and Colin and opened the safe.

Colin sorted through various papers and then located a metal cash box. Inside was a wad of papers that he riffled through until, with a cry of triumph, he found the one with the signature he had been looking for.

Colin was jubilant and took Jonathan out to the police caravan that was now acting as the operational headquarters.

Superintendent Alistair Henderson called in the team charged with documenting all the material in the club as evidence, and was able later to report a highly successful operation to the Commissioner. He carefully avoided mentioning Jonathan. He thought it was really a pity; the young man deserved some recognition, but would never get it. A thought slipped into his mind; the grand lady whose son had left the marker might like to know. Now there was a powerful person, he thought, young Hare would do well to be in her good books.

EIGHTEEN

A Meeting of the Minds

A S THE OPERATION WOUND DOWN, ALISTAIR DECIDED that with Colin and Charmaine around, there might be some awkward questions, so he took himself back to the Yard. He told the team leader to make sure Jonathan was driven back to Oxford.

Jonathan was the centre of some attention, with Colin and Harry actually showing signs of relief. Charmaine was about to make herself scarce when Colin took her elbow and steered her towards Jonathan.

"You owe a lot to Charmaine, you know, she helped us put a tail on the taxi."

Jonathan put out his hand and Charmaine took it; as their hands touched she felt a jolt of pure physical attraction running through her body. Their eyes met and Charmaine blushed as another memory surfaced of that kiss on the dance floor. She took her hand away as if she had been burned. Harry absorbed this with an inner grin; so that's why she'd been so antsy. He'd have to keep an eye on Jonathan; the lad might become even more useful when he understood that he had that other gift. Good job he hadn't cottoned on to it yet; he might behave even more like one of them toffs.

Colin had also observed the encounter and was surprised by a touch of jealousy. Charmaine wasn't a raving beauty, but she somehow managed to make him feel, well, more of a man. He'd better get his mind off that, he thought, although perhaps later?

He turned to Jonathan, saying, "Thanks for the help. I think you'll find that Superintendent Henderson has made things right with Lord Galdraith."

The team leader arrived and took Jonathan away to a car that had far too much power for such an ordinary looking domestic vehicle. The journey back to Oxford reminded him of that trip with Colin across the Yorkshire moors. He was tired when he got back to his Rooms.

When Lord Galdraith was contacted by Superintendent Henderson and briefed on the need for Jonathan's tool case, a number of loose ends that had come out of his discussions with his Lady and those reports from Jason began to fit together. His Scholar had sides to him that the lad had hidden from everybody. Not that they were necessarily bad, just enough to raise his eyebrows. Anyone who ran a large commercial enterprise would have had to use some form of industrial espionage either to gain an advantage or blunt a commercial attack. As far as he could tell, Jonathan had been either sanctioned or pressured into using his special skills. Lord Galdraith found that he was quite proud of his Scholar, not that he could afford to let too many other people know about that side of the young man. And, he recalled, there was still this issue of the document that surfaced at the interview.

Lady Hecate and William had decided to invite Jonathan to dinner.

"Good practice for him, we'll see if he needs coaching on the finer points," said William.

He had thought about how they would raise the subject of the false document and decided not to tell her about the raid on the club.

"When we get to that document, my dear, you'll have to go carefully; he's a bit volatile; walked out on us at the interview; we had to persuade him to come back. Mind you, he did have a point; we treated him badly. Our Proctor rather proved the point that people used to hierarchical control can be unnecessarily harsh with those they think are their inferiors."

Lady Hecate smiled; she had never permitted anyone to treat her harshly, the situation simply didn't arise, but then there were only a few in the land that could claim to be her superiors. And, she thought, *they* didn't need to be harsh; their position was quite sufficient.

When Jonathan opened the door to his Rooms, he found an envelope containing an invitation to attend Lord Galdraith for dinner the next evening at an address that he didn't recognise. He looked it up in the ABC and found it was just a nice walk from the College across a meadow and a footbridge into an obviously higher-class residential area. He couldn't decide from the invitation whether he should wear a dinner jacket. He rang the number and Hilary answered. He was surprised once more at her deference; not the same Hilary that nearly 'had her way with him', he thought with a grin.

Hilary said, "Yes, of course, we always dress, my father insists."

He heard a frostiness, which he thought he preferred to the sexual bantering that he had so misunderstood. But, well, he liked her independence and she had a nice figure. "Will I see you tomorrow?"

There was a silence.

He heard her clear her throat, "Actually, yes, but just for dinner. Apparently I have to make myself scarce after that; you're far too important for me to be included!"

And with that she slammed down the telephone.

The next day the tailors delivered his dinner jacket, so he put it on and examined himself in the mirror. He thought he looked almost as toffee-nosed as those young men gracing the pages of *Tatler*. When he got to the Galdraith residence, Hilary showed him into a reception room of quiet charm. It didn't show any signs of Hilary's taste. As was her usual practice, Lady Hecate had positioned herself to get a first impression of Jonathan without his immediate knowledge; she found this practice to have served her well. But as he entered, she found herself momentarily disconcerted for Jonathan looked far too much like someone in her past.

She struggled to put a name to the shadowy recollection but it escaped her. What she saw was a young man wearing a very presentable dinner jacket, his hair brushed neatly in a rather old-fashioned style; he could have walked out of a page from any society magazine, she thought.

Jonathan was unaware of Lady Hecate's inspection as Lord Galdraith welcomed him and introduced him. She was emanating such charm that he was almost overwhelmed. He had seen her picture somewhere; in one of those glossy magazines probably. He had a vague recollection of a long title, and wasn't she wearing a tiara and huge necklace? Lord Galdraith introduced her as Lady Watchfield. Jonathan sensed that she was a person used to power, but who could wield it with charm, not like some. He sensed that she was there for a purpose.

Hilary was watching with fire behind her eyes; he was acting as if he always moved in these circles. She was exasperated, probably with herself.

Lord Galdraith pulled down his waistcoat. "Don't know why we dress up like this, but Hilary insists, lady of the house now, so we do what she says!"

The Lady laughed, "Why not, you both look so dapper!"

Throughout the dinner, he noticed the Lady observing him. Hilary seemed distracted and took little part in the conversation. Her research on the family crest was driving her crazy. There was a de Quincy daughter, Victoria, who had been to all the right schools; rode horses, of course, not unattractive if her photographs in *Country Life* were anything to go by. It must have been her handwriting on that envelope. Once more she told herself that she had made a social blunder and this added fuel to her anger.

The dinner conversation flowed naturally until Lady Hecate asked one of the usual questions.

"And where does your family come from, Jonathan?"

Jonathan, sensitive as always to the poverty at home, played for time.

"Just a few miles south of here, actually."

Hilary's pent-up anger at Jonathan got the better of her. "Not far from the de Quincys place at Frodsham, I'll bet," she said, as sweetly as she could.

It wasn't often that Lady Hecate was at a loss. The pieces of the puzzle that had been nagging at her suddenly began dancing around in her head, taunting her. She got control of herself.

"You must know the de Quincy family, then, Jonathan," she said with her most dazzling smile. "There's a daughter, Victoria isn't it, pretty girl?"

Jonathan felt betrayed, but had to answer. "Yes, ma'am, Victoria and I met some years ago. I did some work for her father in London and we ran into each other occasionally." He hoped it would do.

"And Lady Antonia?"

"Only once or twice, ma'am."

Perhaps the look on Jonathan's face gave him away, or his tone, but Lady Hecate knew all about Antonia; if Jonathan had got the wrong side of her, that might explain a lot. But something else was there. It was on the edge of her consciousness, something associated with the dinner jacket and the name 'de Quincy'. The image faded as soon as she tried to understand it.

After dinner, Hilary left the room, casting dagger-like glances at Jonathan.

Lord Galdraith took his elbow. "Jonathan, we want to talk to you about a matter of considerable importance. Some of the questions are so sensitive that Lady Watchfield will want to talk to you in private, if you don't mind."

Jonathan wondered what he had done now, and adopted his usual stone face.

Lord Galdraith led off. "I'm sure you recall that unforgivable episode at your interview. It appears there is a reason why that document was sent to us, but we should never have subjected you to it. Would you accept my apologies on behalf of the Master and the College?"

Jonathan had indeed been wondering why the document was sent; that slimy Sir Roger must have sent it, or Sir Hubert, but why? He sensed that there was more to come, so he said nothing.

"I think you already knew about that document. You're a smart young man, but even you couldn't have made our Proctor look so stupid unless you were well prepared."

Jonathan allowed himself a small smile.

"You don't have to tell us, but we would love to know how you knew."

He wondered what to say, and then tried, "My mother has a saying, 'a friend in need is a friend indeed'."

The elegant Lady smiled. "So you had a friend in high places who forewarned you?"

"Yes, ma'am," he said instinctively. He caught the sideways glance between his two interrogators and started to feel nervous.

"Sir, I do value the Scholarship, but I can't see what these questions have to do with it."

More glances were exchanged. Lord Galdraith cleared his throat.

"You're right, Jonathan, and nothing we say here in any way affects your status. If anything, what you have said so far has enhanced it."

Smooth bugger, thought Jonathan.

"But as we looked into that disgraceful document, we found out some disturbing facts; some of them are, well, of great importance. I promise you that whatever is said here won't affect your future."

The Lady made encouraging noises.

But Jonathan had been in traps like this before, deceived by Sir Roger. So his body language was easy to read.

The Lady smiled at Lord Galdraith. "Perhaps it's time for me to talk to him alone, my dear?"

Jonathan, in a very sensitive state, heard a different tone in that last expression – there's something between these two, he thought.

When they were alone, the Lady got up and walked around for a while. She was very graceful, and her presence filled the room. She sat down and looked at him, once more aware of a disconcerting likeness; but to whom? Somewhere in the back of her mind a memory slid in and out of focus. Someone she knew when she was younger, a man with the same way of shielding himself. But the more she struggled the fainter the image became. She took hold of herself, for she had a task to fulfil and this young man might hold the key to her decision.

"Sometimes, Jonathan, events that come together in a person's life place him in a position of great importance without him realising it. That's what has happened to you. I think you know most of this already, but you have chosen not to say anything about it. Let me tell you as much as I understand."

She reached into her handbag and extracted a pair of glasses and a folded piece of paper. Jonathan sensed immediately that it was the 'Statement of Offences'.

She studied it for a while. Jonathan began to be worried.

"I am going to give you my explanation of this disgraceful document, Jonathan. Please understand that it raises some issues that must remain a secret between us."

Jonathan swallowed and nodded.

"I think you were used improperly by Sir Roger and Sir Hubert to carry out a plan that went very wrong."

He couldn't disguise his amazement.

"I believe this plan was of great national importance, and, well, in the balance of things, you were secondary."

Jonathan heard the word 'secondary'; he didn't like the thought of being second to anybody.

She had been observing him closely; so far so good, she thought.

She continued. "It's clear to me that something went wrong with their plan that placed them in personal danger. They think you know what they've done and that is why they took this action."

He started to answer, but she held up her hand.

"Let me continue; did you meet with Sir Roger?" He nodded.

"Did you tell him you knew that he and Sir Hubert were the architects of the plan?"

As she said this, she had a picture of Sir Roger going rigid, reacting to her question about what he and his brother had been up to. The plan was the only thing that fitted all the circumstances.

But Jonathan was shaking his head.

"No, ma'am, it was at Mountbeck in Lord Erinmore's study. There were some papers that Sir Roger gave me to deliver, and then he asked me if I had got over the kidnapping and, well, I thought it was Arthur Salmon, the Gang leader, who had planned it all, so I said that whoever was responsible deserved to be punished."

"Kidnapping?" she said, for once unable to keep the surprise out of her voice.

"Yes, ma'am," he said, not noticing her reaction. "Jane, well Lady Jane I suppose, and I were taken away by car to London. She only came with me at the last minute, so I'm sure that the Gang didn't intend to take her."

She was usually able to conceal her emotions, but this was proving to be too much. She must buy some time.

"I think I would like a drink, Jonathan, perhaps you could get me something?"

He spotted a selection of bottles, but was a bit lost. He saw a stubby dark green bottle with a red seal on it. It announced that it was Tanqueray Gin.

"Gin and tonic, ma'am?" he asked, which was an inspired guess.

"Thank you, Jonathan," she smiled in some surprise.

He slopped a generous amount into a glass and topped it up with tonic water.

She had been watching. "Just perfect," she said, so he brought it over. At her first taste, she knew it was strong, just as she liked it. More to this lad than meets the eye, she thought, laughing to herself.

So the de Quincy brothers had engineered a kidnapping, had they? The full scale of their operation had at last come into focus. She was ready to get back to business.

"Forgive me Jonathan, but I do need to double check. You had no idea that the de Quincy brothers had set up the entire scheme?"

Jonathan had grown much closer to the Lady than he had realised, so he decided to answer more generously than he otherwise would.

"Actually, ma'am, what you say was true at the time. But to be honest, when my friend tipped me off about the document, I worked out that it had to have come from Sir Hubert; it would need his authority to issue it with no DPS number, and I did think that Sir Roger acted strangely that night at Mountbeck. I just thought they'd prepared the document in case I got difficult or something. Of course, when it turned up at the interview, I remembered that Sir Roger and Sir Hubert both knew I was a candidate and I thought they wanted me to fail. I still don't know why they turned against me like that."

She was waiting. Realisation dawned on him, as she recorded the moment.

"If they really did plan the kidnapping." He stopped.

"They couldn't risk it getting out that they had broken the law like that, so they tried to silence me."

They sat for a while. She had brought him to a decisive moment in his life, although he would not realise it for some time to come.

She was thinking that he had some qualities that she could use, and that he certainly had a charm about him; surely he couldn't be as oblivious as he pretended – Victoria agreeing to be friends, how blind could he be. And then there was Hilary, that little firebrand; he had stirred her up too. And what had she heard about that Jane Bellestream girl? Hadn't she had a relapse after some young man had deserted her? Now it seemed that it could well have been Jonathan.

She wondered whether the explanation was more complicated; some men were so focussed on their own future that they couldn't, or wouldn't permit any romantic thoughts to intervene. Jonathan's whole focus was on the Galdraith Scholarship and his university career.

A racing image struck her – one has sometimes to put blinkers on a horse to make it run straighter.

It occurred to her that if she could see how girls were attracted to him, perhaps the de Quincys had also been concerned that Victoria would succumb.

"Let me continue. I have to ask you a personal question first." She waited until he shrugged.

"Tell me what you feel about Victoria."

The question came out of nowhere and he went white, wondering what this had to do with anything.

The Lady reached out and touched his hand. "There's nothing wrong with having feelings for a young and pretty girl. I've seen her pictures in *Country Life* – quite special, I thought."

He sighed. "I've known Victoria for a while, ma'am, we..." He stopped, embarrassed.

After a while, he went on. "We were just friends with nothing in common; she was being pushed by her mother into a society marriage. I suppose that when Sir Roger hired me, we just kept running into each other. But we couldn't even be friends; Lady Antonia put a stop to that."

She heard his bitterness, and asked, "So you were never a threat to steal her away?"

Jonathan couldn't help himself, he laughed out loud. "Steal her away, ma'am; you don't understand, I have nowhere to steal her to!"

It was her turn to be uncomfortable. "I'm sorry if I embarrassed you, but I do need to get at the truth."

She thought he had some secrets that might make interesting investigation, but not now.

"I think you have answered all my questions, Jonathan, thank you. Please listen carefully. What we have talked about tonight must never leave this room, you do understand, I know. You have answered all my questions, but you have not volunteered much. I suspect there are still aspects of this case that would interest me, so, if you ever feel like telling me, let Lord Galdraith know."

She stood and held out her hand. Without thinking about it, he brought his heels together and bowed low as he held her hand very lightly.

She stored away another oddity. William had introduced her by an honorific a long way down her list of entitlements. And yet this young man had demonstrated with his attention to protocol that he understood pretty well what her status was. Remarkable, she thought.

NINETEEN

Ignorance is Bliss

SUPERINTENDENT ALISTAIR HENDERSON LOCKED THE DOOR TO his office. He hoped the memorandum that he was about to write would never see the light of day, for it would set out his interpretation of the events that had caused the Commissioner to be complicit in the attempt to discredit Jonathan Hare. If ever that attempt became public knowledge the damage to the Met would be immense, and too many people were now in the know. He pursed his lips; he suspected that Lady Hecate would by now have complete knowledge as would Lord Galdraith. Colin Davies he could deal with, but Jonathan Hare remained a potential problem. Alistair thought that if an Inquiry was held he could hardly claim innocence. He would send the memorandum to his solicitor to be opened only in specified circumstances. Meanwhile, the least said the better.

As he finished the memorandum, his eyes fell on the envelope containing the marker left by that idiot son of Lady Hecate. He would return it and let the Lady deal with her son. Should he tell her that it was Jonathan who had opened the safe? The lad ought to get some credit, but perhaps it would it be better if his particular clandestine skills remained a secret. Alistair doubted if Lord Galdraith would appreciate other people knowing that his first Scholar was a safe-breaker. No, he thought, better let sleeping dogs lie.

Lady Antonia de Quincy had digested the message that Thomas had delivered. Roger must be in prison; what else could Thomas have meant by 'a secure establishment'? She felt her world crumbling around her. Who would look after her now? With Roger behind bars her social position would be gone and the money would dry up she was sure. Well, she thought, she would have to turn to Rudolph, start a new life. She swept out of Frodsham without a word to Thomas, taking a taxi to Newbury station. Subsequent enquiries would place her there buying a ticket to Paddington, but there the trail would go cold, perhaps for lack of enthusiasm.

Lady Hecate knew she could not put off making her report any longer. She was not happy about it, for although she was sure that Roger and Hubert had crossed the line, there was something else nagging at her, something deeper, something hidden from her. Whatever it was it left her with a sense of sympathy for Roger that belied the facts as she understood them. She decided that her written report would focus on Roger's medical condition which was perhaps enough. The question of introducing the dreadful document was causing her to be uncharacteristically indecisive. Once more she had turned to William for advice.

She had given him a heavily censored version and he had responded that the man had become incapable of handling such difficult affairs.

"Seen it a lot in my world, my dear, men promoted just one rung too high, hang on like grim death, become steadily more, well, 'brittle' is perhaps a good word."

She recalled how secretly pleased she had been with his comment; right on the mark, she had thought. She sent the report by special messenger to the Palace with renewed confidence; but her sense that the story was incomplete would not go away.

When she arrived at the Chief Messenger's palatial office, having been received with the sort of respect that she felt was only her due, she sensed an unusually cool atmosphere. He pretended to read her report, put it aside rather abruptly and steepled his fingers under his chin, examining her closely.

"Perhaps you have underestimated Roger's powers of recovery?"

She gave him her haughtiest glare.

"Perhaps, then, you have not taken into account the high esteem in which he is held?"

It was not necessary for her to be told whose opinion really counted.

"The prevailing view might be that; while everything you have reported is at present irrefutable, Roger deserves at least a period of convalescence with a view to reinstatement should he recover."

She raised her eyebrows, and was about to remonstrate when she thought better of it.

"If that is the prevailing view despite the frailties that I have described, Roger must be owed far more consideration than I expected."

There, she thought, I've put the ball back into their court, best place for it.

She left, feeling that she had done her best, hoping Roger would recover and have learnt a lesson.

Arthur Salmon was arraigned with the rest of the Club staff under his false identity of Percy Thomas. His paperwork was of such an impeccable quality that he felt sure that he could wriggle his way out of this, get a good Brief, claim innocence, just carrying out Joe's orders wasn't he? He was about to apply for bail when he was taken into an office where a senior copper was sitting with a smile on his face.

"Well, Arthur Salmon, did you expect to escape the net?"

Arthur was stunned. Someone had ratted on him, that was clear. And he would never know who had given him away, would he? He could hardly turn to the Gang for help.

"Look, sir," he said as pleasantly as he could. "It's a fair cop, but you know what the Gang will think. If you put me in the clink with them, I'll be dead in a week. I'll plead guilty to whatever you say, but only under my new name and if you'll put me somewhere away from them."

Alistair grinned. It wasn't such a bad idea at that; Arthur could be a prime source of information; the boys in Sterling Control would get his secrets out of him and think it was an early Christmas present. And perhaps all wasn't lost concerning the American. Surely Arthur would know something helpful.

Alistair looked down at the beautifully doctored paperwork and smiled. "Well, Percy, perhaps we can work something out after all."

Colin Davies was informed of the decision to allow Sir Roger a period of recuperation although he would have to give up his position. A replacement was now being sought urgently. He wasn't surprised but began to feel that his own days were numbered. What he had learned about the document from Reggie had unsettled him; he couldn't go along with what the brothers had done. Good job he had kept in with Alistair Henderson; he would apply, even if it meant going back to his previous rank. Meanwhile he had another problem. Thomas at Frodsham had reported that Lady Antonia had simply disappeared. He'd had to tell Miss Victoria and she hadn't taken it well. She'd retired to her room and hadn't been heard from for hours.

Back in Eaton Square Lady Hecate was lying in bed, saddened by so much of what she had learnt. She thought about the passing of the old standards, gradual as a receding tide. Time was when men stood by their word, and knew what was just and fair, when Ministers resigned if their departments made serious mistakes instead of being forced out by public outcry. Once, a man's honour was important, and a nation's integrity was forged on the moral strength of its leaders.

She understood as well as anyone that, from time to time, difficult decisions were made on the basis of the 'lesser evil'. If she were free to talk about it she would cite the bombing of Coventry and the tragic loss of its cathedral and so many lives. Our leader had had a choice; warn the citizens and let the Reich know we had broken their high command codes, or let the raid go ahead.

But Roger and Hubert had acted out of personal interest. She could excuse them for using Jonathan as bait, but not for treating him so viciously just to protect themselves and family ambitions. She shuddered as Lady Antonia came to mind. The country owed Roger such a favour for stepping in like that, but the woman was, well, no better than she should be. She had never even given Roger the heir he so badly needed. An avenue of thought opened; it was shadowy and before she could grasp it, it had faded away.

It was clear to her that Roger was already suffering from guilt when he met with Jonathan at Mountbeck – she wondered briefly what papers he could have been delivering – otherwise he would never have assumed that Jonathan knew that he and Hubert had conspired to place him in harm's way. The lad had naturally assumed that the Gang leader had been the guilty party. And for the two of them to concoct that document was, well, quite beyond the pale, Roger had suffered a just reward and as for Hubert, she would exact some retribution, even use up some of her Palace favours.

As she dozed, some imagery flowed into her mind, from a poem perhaps, in which the floodtide of faith and moral strength and decency was receding, leaving behind the grinding pebbles of materialism, where ends always justified the means and where there was no joy in honour. What had been washed and clean was now but detritus, and all was darkness, where ignorant armies were clashing in the night.

TWENTY

The White Knight

JONATHAN'S TELEPHONE RANG. IT WAS JASON.

"Oh, you are back, sir, could you ring this number, it's urgent."

Inspector Colin Davies sounded as unsettled as Jonathan could recall.

"Mr. Hare, I wouldn't bother you, but we have a situation here. Miss Victoria is very upset; there have been developments since we last spoke; very serious, I'm afraid. Miss Victoria..."

He started again, "Well, if you could come perhaps we can retrieve something from this mess!"

Martin met him at Paddington, and was silent for a while, and then said, "Not good news for the family, and especially Miss Victoria, sir. Better for you to hear it from the Inspector, he seems to be in charge now."

So Jonathan arrived fearing the worst and listened to Colin Davies tell him that Sir Roger had been admitted to a very private clinic, no visitors at all, no indication of when he might be released. Lady Antonia had been seen briefly at Frodsham and seemed to have abandoned the family altogether.

"It gets worse; this place is tied to the appointment held by Sir Roger and since he can no longer fulfil the duties, the family will have to return to Frodsham."

Jonathan was stunned. "What about Victoria? Can I see her?"

Colin told him she had asked to see him immediately he arrived, "But first you needed to know how serious the situation is."

Colin led the way and knocked on a bedroom door. They heard Victoria's voice and went in. Jonathan thought she looked as bad as she did in the room at the Society where they celebrated after the raid on the warehouse. He hadn't known then that she had just broken off her engagement. He managed to keep his face blank. She was fully dressed, but her face was a mess, with her mascara smeared and her hair falling out of an attempt to comb it straight back, not her most flattering style, he thought.

Colin stood around for a moment, but left the room, saying, "Be downstairs if you need me."

Jonathan put his arms around her and she immediately burst into tears. She sobbed for some time, and then broke away.

"What is happening to me, Jonathan? It's just one disaster after another. If I didn't have you..."

She paused, perhaps realising what she had said.

"As a friend, I mean," she continued hurriedly, "what would I do?"

"Come on, Victoria, let's go for a walk."

They went down into the garden, holding hands, and every now and then she wiped her eyes. He couldn't think how to express himself. He had begun to understand that women didn't deal with problems the way he did. His brain worked to a linear logic and intuitive leaps were a mystery to him.

He knew what she should do; no, he thought, I know what *I* would do.

It was a moment in his life that passed without conscious recognition – he would have to get her to work out the best course, even if it wasn't the one he would have chosen.

They sat down in the twilight and she leaned against him.

"Let me tell you a story," he said. "There was once a young lad who met a pretty young lass. She invited him to visit her in her magical kingdom, so he mounted his trusty steed and rode out to meet her there.

But her mother did not welcome him, for the lass was really a princess who must marry a prince. So their friendship came to an end. But he often thought about her in her magical kingdom. Then one day at her father's castle, they met again. He was just a tradesman serving her father, and she was betrothed to a prince. But they remembered each other. The lad, a bit older now, went off to war for her father and never expected to see her again."

She was shaking, whether from laughter or tears he couldn't decide.

"Go on," she whispered.

"One day, when he had come back from the war, she summoned him to her magical kingdom. She was in distress, her prince had been a coward and she would not marry him. The young man by then had won honour and fame and had a new King to serve. So he could only offer her friendship while he fought new wars and took on new challenges. Then she summoned him again to her father's castle. Her father was ill and couldn't look after his castle. The young man didn't know what to do until he thought of her magical kingdom and how wonderful it was there. So he took her there and she became the Lady of the Magical Kingdom."

He was proud of this concoction, but she hadn't responded. She sat up and looked at him. "And that's it? You can't stop there, how does it end?"

He looked at her.

"I don't know, Victoria; perhaps, when he has served the new King, he will come back to the magical kingdom, perhaps another Knight will come and capture the fair Lady."

She snorted, "And why would the princess wait around for a Knight who just wants to fight wars?"

They both laughed, and he said, with a huge shrug, "That's what Knights do!"

She hugged him. "That was such a nice story, Jonathan, it reminded me of Tennyson – *Idylls of the King*, you know."

He admitted that perhaps it wasn't totally original. "What do you think, though, Victoria?" he asked.

She seemed to have recovered, for she got up and said, "I'll tell you in the morning."

Victoria was in her room, getting ready for bed. She was feeling better, but wondering about Jonathan. For such a terribly focussed person, with such an interest in mechanical and masculine things, he had suddenly demonstrated an almost poetic side. She had been enthralled by the story; it was so romantic that she had only grasped the relevance towards the end. But he had signalled clearly that she would have to wait for him. Perhaps her father would recover and her mother would return. Then she realised that she had no wish to go back to her old life, it was far too constraining.

And, she decided, she didn't want Jonathan arranging her life for her, either; from now on she would direct her own future. She lay back with a look of determination that would have surprised Jonathan had he been there to see it.

When she dreamed, it was of a Lady waiting in her turret, looking always for her Knight to come, but when he came he was escorting a younger woman of noble birth, all dressed in white.

Lady Hecate had received the marker with a note from the superintendent. She was so relieved to get the evidence of her son's disgraceful conduct that she put the note to one side. She smiled to herself and decided that she would keep the marker as a surety against his future behaviour. Eventually she read the note. Alistair had decided that Jonathan deserved some credit if only anonymously and had written "We were fortunate that the expert in safe-breaking could be persuaded to undertake the task." It would be several hours before the phrase 'expert in safe-breaking' began to nag at Lady Hecate. When she finally connected it to the Statement of Offences document, she had to sit down. Surely not, she thought, surely not.

Jonathan was having breakfast when Victoria came into the dining room. She was wearing a dress that floated as she walked. She was looking much better, made up well and with her hair arranged in a more flattering style. She got some toast and sat down opposite him. They smiled at each other, and he told her she was looking more like her old self.

"Like a pretty lass in a magical kingdom?" she teased.

They looked at each other, knowing there was more to say.

She was the first to speak. "Tell me what's so magical about Frodsham, Jonathan."

He was relieved that his suggestion seemed to have worked, so he grinned at her. "Well for a start it's only an hour or so from Oxford by trusty steed."

She chewed on some toast. "Less than that by the Rolls."

He was waiting for a resolution, but was now sensible enough not to force the issue.

"The Inspector told me yesterday that my father will have to leave here. I always thought he owned it, the Society just a hobby. And he will need somewhere to go when they send him home."

He kept tight control of himself.

"So I have decided that I will go and get Frodsham prepared for him."

Her chin was pushed slightly forward, her eyes fixed on him.

"What a good idea!" he said enthusiastically. She snorted and got up.

As she was leaving, she looked over her shoulder. "Don't wait too long to saddle your trusty steed," she said, with a toss of her head.